KENDRAI MEEKS

MISTRESS
OF
CINDERS

ENTER THE KINGDOM

Dedicated to the innovators,
educators, and imagination
explorers.

San Francisco

2148

ONE

SOME GAMES WERE WORTH WINNING, even if you had to walk down the stairs, past the damp walls, and through floating cobwebs to play them.

Cindira shivered, but it wasn't because of the misty, mildewy kiss of air blowing across her forehead. "You know if we ever get trapped down here when there's a tsunami, we're both dead, right?"

Unlike the Ferries, the Stadium had to keep up the appearance of being a legitimate business. If you wandered in at the right time of day, their burgers and fries weren't too bad. Assuming you didn't think too much about what meat you were actually eating. Raids, if unusual, happened. Generally, whenever the Authority got a new chief or some semi-celebrity chiphead jacked out for the last time, sparking seasonal outcry and tissue paper tears. The Stadium, consequently, kept its jackpods under the bar. Literally. Storage closets on the north and south side of the joint concealed hidden staircases leading to twin dank cellars just large enough to host two devices each. Cindira had always suspected there were more, but she'd never had a reason to go looking.

"Tsunami?" At her back, Scotia scoffed. "A basement in San Francisco, and ocean levels still on the rise? I'm surprised this isn't an aquarium already." The redhead nudged her friend forward with a gentle push on the shoulder. "It's a good thing we won't be down here too long, then. I checked this guy's stats. His completion average comes in just a little under four minutes."

"Is that typical?"

Scotia scoffed. "Asked like a woman who hasn't been with a man in a while."

"Hey, this has nothing to do with that." Cindira flicked on the light switch when she was the first to reach the bottom. "You know why I don't date anymore. Every time a guy finds out who my parents are, then all they see when they look at me is them, not *me*."

Scotia didn't understand what it was like. It didn't matter that she was plain looking or didn't have her family's money or that she wasn't constantly talked about on the celebrity gossip streams like her stepsiblings were. Cindira was a Tieg, even if only in name. More importantly, she was Omala Grover's only child. Once a man discovered your mother had invented the platform for saving the world from destruction and your father had monetized it to make sinful amounts of money from it after their divorce, you became a two-dimensional trinket to them. Suddenly, they weren't dating Cindy, that shy but smart girl from the coding department. They were dating Cindira Tieg, and her legacy, no matter how unwanted, became the other woman in their relationship.

THE CYRSTALINES GLOWED a soft green, reflecting off the semi-opaque lids of the two jackpods. "Four minutes is damned fast. Are you sure I can beat that?"

"If I thought you'd lose, I wouldn't have put ten thousand greens on you."

"Ten thousand—" Shock cut off the coder's words. "That's a hell of purse. You sure that much crypto won't cull attention?" If the transaction had been in kartz or rubis, she wouldn't worry. While not technically illegal, tracing the transactions through the neo-c blockchain was a task only the most talented of fiscal hackers could handle.

"Sorry, babe, I only have the regular kind of crypto. And you of all people should know that 10K isn't enough to raise any eyebrows in this town."

"Isn't it what you pay in rent each month *in this town*?"

Scotia shook her head. "Not this month. Not unless you win, that is."

In so many ways, Scotia was everything Cindira was not. Beautiful where she was plain. Courageous where she was timid. Opportunistic where she was passive. She was also the only reason Cindira had the courage to show up in at a place like this. Hackdomes were a clear violation of her contract with Plaxis. Something about its elite tier of code writers using their skills in environments it didn't own.... When Scotia was around, no one paid much attention to plain, little

Cindira Tieg. No one ever noticed, therefore, the keen resemblance she bore to the vreal's patron saint and its most famous martyr.

A martyr she might follow in death, if an earthquake hit and the building pancaked into the basement.

Scotia must have read the anxiety written in Cindira's features. She wrapped a hand around the young woman's shirt and pulled her along.

"I promise," she said, "if the water starts pouring in, I'll hit the emergency shut down and get you out of here. I'll even throw you over my shoulder and carry you out if I need to."

"But don't forget to get our winnings on the way out, okay?"

Scotia turned back over her shoulder, giving Cindira a *Who in the hell do you think I am?* look.

Two ancient devices occupied the room, fourth generation or worse, each sprouting wires from its underside like weeds. Officially, they were called NNIPs, or Neural Network Interface Pods. "Jackpod" was the colloquial term, but the truly cynical used more morbid terms. Meat locker, crypt, sarcos, chippers... If you didn't know you were in the basement of a hackdome, you might think you'd just ended up in an Egyptian tomb. Except for the fact that the devices had transparent walls and a cranial interlink shield that looked like an upside-down pasta drainer cut in half, the similarity couldn't be overstated. On the opposite end of the bar, her opponent would be shimmying into his own device, getting ready for battle. Cindira needed to do the same.

Scotia tried to calm Cindira's nerves with levity. "Already for you, Sleeping Beauty."

The coder grimaced as she used a small step stool to climb up into the device. "Any sign of water, right?"

It was ridiculous. This wasn't the Ferries. There were no dilapidated buildings in this part of town, now halls full of wasted chipheads, offering any part of their body, real or vreal, for just enough crypto to get them jacked up another hour. Cindira thought it might have been in the Ferries and other underground cyberdens like them that the jackpods got their most infamous moniker: coffins. Chipheads jacked in, and if their wallets allowed for it, never jacked out. In the vreal, problems were few and opportunities for diversion, great. In the years after war had uploaded, the government had been all too happy to encourage their addiction, the theory being that experts in vreal immersion could make prime soldiers in the wardomes outside Gaia's capital city someday. What had they been thinking, Scotia would say? The chipheads didn't even fight for their own prosperity, why would they fight for their countries? Especially given that most of the countries who fought their wars in Gaia hadn't even existed fifty years ago.

Sure, hackdomes were looked upon by the digi-elite as plebian, but the Stadium was a legitimate business. Its owner, Talia Green, wouldn't risk getting shut down—or worse— by letting one of her regular champions drown.

Despite only being a year older, Scotia knew how to summon a comforting smile any mother would recognize. No doubt a skill that came in handy for a Social Worker.

"The smallest drop, and I'll eject you."

Cindira tried to ignore the smell of sweat and trace amounts of urine that clung to the inside of the jackpod. These low level vreals and standard jackpods didn't have sophisticated enough source code to carry over physical pain from the vreal into reality. If they had, Cindira would have been a convicted murderer many times over by now. That didn't mean the brain and body never reacted to something inside the platform.

So far, Cindira had never felt that kind of fear. The vreal was the only place she controlled everything, where she had real power. She'd never lost a match. Why would she fear anything? She sat back and nodded to Scotia to close the lid. Cindira reached up, looking for the launch button that would turn on the neural interface and turn off her interaction with the real.

The game was afoot, and she was ready.

BLACK WISPS SPIRALED in a distant gray sky, but both the weight and balance of the form in which she found herself felt alien. The massive hands shouldn't surprise her, but platforms that forced her to embody someone so different from her true self always disorientated. There was never any telling the form you would take in the hackdome. Most battle programs like this one came preinstalled with a catalog, and the avatar you found yourself in was usually up to chance. Today, she was what Scotia liked to refer to as "the Banshee." If this creature had existed in the real world, it would stand about two meters, with arms about two-thirds the length of its body. Other than that, though, scrawny. Little muscle mass, and a profile which did not lend itself to agility or speed. Neither of those things mattered, though. What dominated the hackdomes wasn't physical strength, though too many players fell into the trap of internalizing what they thought the shape of their avatar demanded. But this was a realm of algorithms and logic, and the only muscle a champion needed to flex was their intelligence.

Deep breaths through her mouth acclimated Cindira's native neural processes to the faux experiences, as well as let her call to arms her... well, arms. Around her feet lay a ramshackle collection of tools and weapons: lumber, axe blades, rope, spears, stones, swords of varying shapes and sizes... a mirror image to those that her foe would have. Straw bales formed a wall around them, both to force the fight into tight quarters, and to simplify the virtual platform's speed and performance. The system read the code the player thought, stringing together the tools provided into weapons of choice. Outside of this manipulation, real world rules still held. Gravity couldn't be overwritten. Day would not become night. The dead didn't come back to life.

The one left standing at the end won, in whatever way that came to pass.

Overhead, horns blared, and within two blinks, her opponent's avatar took shape across the arena. Only by seeing her enemy could she truly see herself, for what united also divided. Each had the same goal; to conquer.

"Mistress of Cinders." He didn't look at her when he spoke, instead leaning over to take up one of the staffs from his armory. "Finally, a worthy competitor."

"I didn't catch your handle."

Cindira kept her eyes fixed on him as he leaned the staff against his shoulder while testing the weight of a grapefruit-sized wedge of rock in his hand. A show, of course. Neither would forget that back in the Stadium, the crowd watching on the aeroprojectors hurried to get their bets registered before one of the competitors made the first strike. No doubt the odds had shifted towards her foe; too many spectators accepted the weaker-looking female form she occupied as inherently disadvantaged. Luckily, Scotia wouldn't be one. She'd take every bet, no matter how small or how large.

"I'm called Barrel. I'm not sure why, but that's all part of the mystique, isn't it?"

"Barrel?" She searched her memory and found it wanting. "I don't remember seeing you on any of the master boards at the Stadium before."

"It's my first time."

That didn't sound right. "You have to earn your way into the Master's League."

"I did, or should I say, you earned my place for me."

Her head cocked to the side, the flow of long, shinny blue hair flowing around her shoulders.

Barrell passed along a smirk as he looked up. "You've beaten everyone else. I was... let's just say 'recruited.'" He strained as he familiarized himself with the balance of his newly-coded weapon, an impressive meld of axe blade to long staff that reminded Cindira of the Grim Reaper's sickle. "Best of battle to you, Mistress."

"And to you." She returned the customary salutation moments before he ran for her at full force, the staff pulled back to his right side.

He might as well have been narrating his attack.

Barrel swung only seconds after Cindira stepped to her left, giving his axe nothing but air to rend. Speed turned against him as his center of gravity shifted. Her adversary fell to the ground in a *harrumph*, barely avoiding the bite of his own weapon.

Barrel bellowed. "Coward! Diving away from an attack."

"I stepped away from an *attempted* attack," she returned. "You think the rules are different here? They're not. *The supreme art of war is to subdue the enemy without fighting.* Was true when Sun Tzu said it thousands of years ago. It's still true now, even in a virtual arena."

In a flash, Barrel regained his feet. "Thanks for the philosophy lesson, let me give you one in anatomy."

The swing came quicker this time, so much so that Cindira found it difficult to maneuver her avatar's bulk away. Barrel kept a striking distance, supplemented by a step. He was a quick learner, she'd give him that. Unlikely he'd try running at her full force again.

She needed a weapon, but the opponent lay between her armaments and herself, and only the wall of haystacks lay behind her. *Those* weren't weapons, but it didn't mean they were useless. He'd need to be closer, though.

Cindira put up her empty hands as she sidled back, drawing him by instinct in her direction. "The fight seems unfair, given that I'm unarmed." Her back hit the boundary.

"You had as much time to choose a weapon as I did." He pulled back his staff again. "Or maybe you don't know the simple code it takes to weave together wood, metal, and rope. I can teach you – for a price. *Hyuah!*"

Dry shafts of grass scratched her fingers as she pulled the straw bale behind to her front. Barrel's weapon anchored deep within, the curvature of the blade a disadvantage, catching the bound stack that now gained strength in its formation. With one vigorous yank, Cindira took Barrel's weapon from his hands, throwing the impaled bale to the far end of the arena.

"There." She rubbed her palms down the front of her shirt. "Now we're even again."

Red-faced, Barrel guffawed. "You... cheated! The bales aren't weapons!"

"Everything here is a weapon, if you figure out a way to use it. The wall's held together by a weak repeating code, but it's easily undone. I could teach you – for a price."

"Why, you—"

His response came too suddenly for her to dodge. The force of his blow knocked Cindira from her feet. Strong, angry hands encircled her throat. Left, right, up... no direction offered solace. Maybe she had been wrong. Maybe *brawn* would win over brain.

Virtual death didn't affect the real-world body, but the mind still felt the pain. Stars burst around the edges of her vision, blackness creeping in. She might as well surrender; her dead body would only up Scotia's losses. But the movement of something on the edge of her vision drew Cindira's attention. A flash of white fur, the scurry of tiny feet. Some sort of rodent? She'd never seen one in the arena before, but then again, she'd never been pinned to the ground, moments from defeat.

The creature was gone, but it had drawn her eyes to the only thing that could save her now: the stockade of weapons she'd ignored earlier. What she wouldn't give now for one of the swords, or even an axe. If wishes were weapons, Barrel would fall down dead. But no code she knew of could make things fly through the air.

"Why won't you yield, already?" Barrel's grip clenched even tighter. "You should be dead!"

The dead did not wage war. Cindira struggled to make her muscles obey, drawing up her left hand to signal while her brain attempted to piece together the necessary lines of code that would tell the program she'd surrendered. Barrel's grin widened, but only for a scant moment. The very next, his eyes filled with terror. Suddenly his hands were off her as he backed away.

"What in the hell?"

Cindira sat up, sputtering, spinning around to follow her opponent's gaze, when she too saw it. Every weapon, every blade, every staff, even the fist-sized rocks, floated in the air, poised to strike.

She blinked, and every one of them rushed forward, streaming through the air. Cindira swallowed her scream and squeezed her eyes shut. To victor was one thing. To disseminate your opponent limb from limb was quite another.

"JESUS CHRIST, CINDIRA, get out! Get out of that, quick!"

Cindira opened her eyes, seeing not the bloody gore she'd just caused, but the hood of the jackpod lifting away.

Smoke stained the air as she sat up, looking around in confusion, trying to find the source of the heat against her face. Had the jackpod overheated? She couldn't move fast enough. Adrenaline pumping through her veins pushed her to her feet and into Scotia's hold. The redhead pulled Cindira clear as white fogged the air. A bartender bearing a fire hydrant rushed past, followed by the surly gamemaster who managed the floor.

"No winner!" He threw his hands wildly through the air. "System error! No winner! All bets void!"

The crowd groaned, some shouting that Cindira had clearly been defeated, others saying that she had been on the edge of turning the tide.

Confusion clouded Cindira's thoughts. "Scotia?"

"You heard him, system error." The redhead didn't pause, too concerned with making the door. "Weapons don't just fly through the air unless something goes wrong. Hurry up, we have to get out of here before anyone tries to claim you were cheating. I don't know who the hell this Barrel is, but he was seconds away from making a half mill off your defeat."

"So what? He didn't lose anything. You heard the gamemaster, all bets void."

"I don't care. A man who can throw that kind of black market crypto at the Stadium isn't someone we want knowing who we really are."

Scotia may not have been alone in her thinking. As normality reclaimed her and Cindira became more in tune with her real-world surroundings, she found herself in a stream of people heading to the exit, though that also could be because the smell of smoke filled the air.

"Glitches happen," she tried to argue, looking back over her shoulder in hopes of catching a glimpse of someone befitting the name Barrel. "I'm sure it's really not that big... of a... d—"

Her words died when she saw him: Cade Fife, staring back at her with equal doses of cockiness and condescendence.

So, Johanna had sent a spy again. How typical. Just what her father's second wife thought she'd discover, Cindira didn't want to imagine. Maybe an excuse to fire her. As if her father, Rex, would ever let that happen. Hell, as if Kaylie, Johanna's daughter and Cindira's stepsister, would. Who would code Kaylie's dresses, design her carriages, do all the work inside the company that Kaylie took credit for? Whatever Cade might think he'd uncovered, getting into a verbal standoff with "Barrel" wasn't in her interest on any level. The Stadium was one of the few places she could come and be who she was without hiding it, ironically, but hiding it all behind Scotia.

Cindira felt the need to be gone ASAP, outpacing Scotia in three steps and pulling her friend insistently forward by the hand.

"You're right. Let's get the cache out of here."

BY THE TIME THEY SLOWED down, it was only because they had run out of land. Here, on the bay shore, the red-blue shafts of lights from the Authority transports no longer lit the sky. Across the murky waters, over a field of makeshift boats bobbing in the water, the barren Berkeley Hills rose. Further down, an eerie red glow marked where the Ferries stood, housing who-knew-how-many chipheads, vreal addicts who'd given up on any chance at life and instead slowly drifted further into their fantasies.

"I think we're good." Cindira's words pushed past airy breaths. "If anyone thought we were worth tagging, they'd have caught up to us by now. But we still don't have much time."

Cindira lifted her comque into view, tapping away at the light-based interface it projected.

Doubled over, Scotia scrunched up her nose. "What are you doing?"

She waited until the task was complete to answer. "I pinned into the Authority's mainframe, made sure your comque GPS records were altered." She lowered her wrist, and automatically, the light green glow from the wrist-worn device died away. "And gave you about twenty minutes to get home before your GPS node reactivates."

Scotia's eyes went wide. "You can do that?"

Cindira shrugged. "Their AI isn't too different from what we use at Plaxis, and it operates with the Purusha Plus language as its backbone, so yeah." Her eyes rolled to the side. "Not that it wasn't without consequence."

Head dropping, Scotia forced her breath into submission before pushing off her knees and pulling herself erect. "Do I want to know?"

"If we weren't there tonight, no way we could have won the tournament, is there?"

"Jesus, Mary and..." Snapping to attention, Scotia shook her head. "At least tell me you retracted our entry fee?"

"What do you think I am, some backstreet hacker?"

"No, you're main street, biggest storefront. The best of the best." A smile on Scotia's face fell away. "They announce the new Director tomorrow, don't they?"

"It's going to be Kaylie." She'd said it so plainly, it sounded like an announcement. "At least, everyone says it's going to be. I don't know; no one told me anything definitive."

"Which means it's not going to be you," Scotia said. "Even though you're obviously the best person for the job. That whole department rides on your back."

Cindira shook her head. "That's not true. There are a dozen coders working in the Kitchens. If I fell off the map tomorrow, the only one who'd care would be Kaylie, and then only because I couldn't be at her beck and call anymore. Then who would create all the dresses she wears in the Kingdom that she's so famous for?"

"I still don't get that. Does she even keep them on long enough to be seen by more than one person?"

Both women laughed until Scotia sobered. "It's not fair, the way she uses you and claims credit for all your best work."

No, it wasn't, but it was the tradeoff Cindira was willing to make. Managers were by consequences ambassadors and politicians. Cajoling and manipulation weren't powerful tools in Cindira's arsenal. Not unless it had to do with making the code obey her command. Kaylie was a much better woman for the job. Not only because she had those abilities, but because she seemed to thrive on exercising them. Dislike the personality traits though she might, Cindira couldn't deny the benefits she reaped from Kaylie's weaseling. In some ways, her stepsister had become her shield. The last thing Cindira wanted was to be in the public eye again. The coder still remembered what that was like when her famous mother had been found floating in the waters off the coast of San Francisco. It was so easy for sympathy to drift into expectation. Cindira never wanted to be at the business end of someone else's best intentions again.

This time when Cindira twisted her hand to display her comque, lighting the time with three taps, it was for Scotia's benefit. "Nineteen minutes now. Can you do it or not? Every time I push into the system to change something, it creates ripples, and too many ripples turn into waves. I have limits, you know."

"Liar. I just saw what you did in that hackdome. Don't think I'll be forgetting about *that* soon." Scotia placed fisted hands on her hips and looked up the street, back the way they'd fled. "I can do it. I'll be dead and sweaty as a hog when I get home, but I can do it. It's only running a kilometer uphill, right?" She tapped Cindira on the shoulder. "We'll get them next time, and then, drinks on me."

"Out of my winnings?"

"I mean, it only seems fair, right?" The redhead smiled, assumed the ready stance, then started her jog. She was only a few steps away when, trotting in place, she turned back to the coder. "Did you notice that it wasn't Authority conducting the raid?"

Cindira's face screwed up. "I didn't stop to look." She traced her memory, but she wasn't sure she had seen any of the uniformed agents in the bar. Her focus had been on getting out. "Who was it then?"

"If I didn't know better, I'd say it was Gaian Royal Real Guard."

That didn't make any sense. Gaia operated as a sort of independent monarchical democracy, and its head of state, bona fide. That being said, in the real, the prince didn't have much more than security staff to guard the complex where his offices, residence, and jackpod bays were located. Why pull from such a limited stock to raid something as mundane as The Stadium?

"That *is* weird." Cindira huffed. "But not my monkeys, not my circus. Now go. I'm not committing a second international hacking crime tonight to save your ass."

TWO

CINDIRA OBSERVED HER father's second wife from the only acceptable position: at a distance. Standing at the back of the crowd came with other benefits, though. Best of which was that no one noticed you, and the last thing she wanted today was to be noticed. Already, it felt like the secret of her narrow escape the night before had taken on mass, a bowling ball imbedded in the pit of her stomach that should make everyone gawk at her.

So far, though, so good. As Kaylie gloated at the right hand of her own mother, none of the Plaxis employees in the lobby had a vantage from which to notice Cindira's angry frown. Perhaps Johanna, standing at the front, *could* have noticed, if she ever cared to lend a sympathetic eye. Sadly, the only time her stepmother gave her any consideration was when barking out commands or passive-aggressive insults.

It was better to be ignored than admonished.

"There was a healthy crop of candidates, both from outside and within Plaxis, worthy to fill the vacant Director of Code Integrity and Specialization position." Bold, blond, and voluptuous, Johanna also had a tongue forked in the middle, even if metaphorically. "At the end of the day, the candidate who embodied our ideals, was a proven leader, and has shown herself to be not only competent but cerebral in the broadening and emboldening of our platforms, became obvious. Yes, she *is* also my daughter, but Kaylie's innovation to create vreal estate *within* the Kingdom environment itself has led to our biggest quarterly growth of profits since we launched fifteen years ago."

Cindira became a block of ice, even as Scotia leaned over, keeping her voice to a whisper. Barely.

"Weren't those *your* ideas?"

"And my code that made them possible," Cindira replied. She wouldn't mention how her marketing plans, saved in her company e-folder until she worked up the courage to show them to her father, had somehow ended up in Johanna's inbox branded with Kaylie's name.

Plaxis's Executive Vice-President droned on. "Kaylie also understands that, while we still hold a dominant share of the luxury VR environment market, our competition increases not only by the day, but by the hour. Tagentry and others like them are keeping us on our toes, however. Each of their innovations inspires us to push for our own."

Or hire out the competition's best assets or sue for infringement, Cindira thought wryly. Not that the second strategy ever got very far. It wasn't like the other vreal platformers were stealing Plaxis's source code. How could they, when Plaxis itself didn't have access to it? It was a testament to Omala Grover's genius that her coding was so robust it was still holding up fifteen years later. *Mostly.* Luckily, the Kitchens ("Where the best code is cooked!") knew how to work the derivative programming language that Cindira's mother had invented well enough to patch up the problems that crept up from time to time. For now.

"We need to improve our existing products and create those that will take us into the future," Johanna continued. "The Kingdom must endure, not for its own sake, but for the sake of humanity. Never forget: it makes possible Plaxis's continued and independent support of Gaia. Yes, one may be the playground of the rich and famous, but the other is the salvation of the poor and voiceless."

Only years of practice kept Cindira from rolling her eyes. Her mother's legacy and gift to humanity meant little to her stepmother. There were only two things Johanna longed for: power and money, preferably other people's. If not for her father's controlling interest in the company, Cindira was certain Plaxis would have pulled its support of Gaia long ago. Even after all the good the platform had done, taking warfare into the virtual world and curbing the destruction of both the environment and societies, Johanna thumbed her nose at its continued existence.

At least, behind closed doors. Literally. How many times, while home from boarding school or university on summer break, had she overheard her stepmother's condescension?

Scotia squeezed her shoulder. "Don't worry. She won't last."

"Kaylie's savvy." Cindira turned to her friend. "As long as she produces results and keeps the Kingdom growing, she'll stay in that position."

Besides, Cindira couldn't visualize the situation in which Johanna would ever fire her own daughter.

"You mean as long as she has you there to clean up her crappy code." Scotia shook her head.

No doubt about that. Over the last three years, from the moment Cindira returned to the city where she'd been born, Kaylie had done as little as possible, and sloppily at that. Cindira cleaned up the messy code and made it actually work. Because Kaylie was her boss, and because her one true talent was swaying people to believe in her own righteousness, she got all the credit. Because Cindira feared the fallout of going against her stepfamily and upsetting her father in the process, she let her.

Scotia continued. "Call her out."

Cindira shook her head. "Kaylie's the celebrity face of Plaxis. I'd be doing more damage to the company than helping myself. Besides, no one except you and the Kitchen crew would believe me, and they're not going to do anything that would cost them their jobs."

"You're amazing. How can you go into the arena like you did last night and kick serious ass but still turn belly up for the Fifes? Next time you sit down to your station, code yourself a new backbone."

"This isn't the vreal, Scotia." Cindira kept her voice low. "There, I can be whoever I want to be. Here, I'm just plain, little Cindira Tieg."

Scotia swallowed a frustrated laugh. "Just because you can't code the walls here doesn't mean you couldn't knock them down if you tried. If you keep letting Kaylie take advantage of you, you're going to make her CEO someday. You need to stand up for yourself. Doctor's orders."

"I'm not sure having a PhD in social work qualifies you to—"

"It does."

Her friend cut her off, and probably would have launched into her boilerplate synopsis of how Cindira's so-called family needed a professional intervention, if she didn't suddenly tug her friend three feet to the left. Scotia tucked a pointed finger against the side of her face, indicating a man who leaned against the wall, near where Plaxis's "royal family" was holding court.

"Shut the front door, who is *that*?"

The stranger stood out, and not just because he was handsome. Such men were a dime a dozen, given Plaxis's affluent clientele and the ease of synth surgery for those of means. His face had a certain level of imperfection that suggested he hadn't been altered. One eyebrow arced a few degrees higher, a tiny bump on the side of his nose kept him from the type of unnatural symmetry the altered had.

Like Kaylie, for example.

Cindira folded her arms and grimaced. "You want to win some crypto? Put greens down on that either being Kaylie's conquest du jour, or her next target."

Her stepsister wore men like some women wore shoes. Only, this guy, whoever he was, wasn't Kaylie's typical fare. He dressed like a man who hoped not to be noticed. With his slate-colored suit, pressed white shirt, black leather belt, and solid black tie, he'd mastered a monochrome palate. The scheme had backfired here, though. Plaxis employees were encouraged to dress in the bright, flashy styles of the social elite to give clients the impression that they were "not only welcome to join the Kingdom, but already part of it." It was good marketing, and Cindira couldn't argue against its wisdom, but it did often give her the impression that she was walking through a Carnivale celebration instead of an office building.

In fact, the only other one dressed to sink into the background in the room... was her.

He stood at the front of the lobby, but at the sidelines of the crowd, a line of sight kept fixed on Johanna and the employees milling about. She recognized the tactic. From there, he could observe without any suspicion of tactical intent.

"I swear I've seen him somewhere before." Scotia leaned to the side, vying for a better view. "Is he a member of the board?"

Cindira shook her head. "I know the board members." They were frequent guests in her father's home, not to mention luminaries in the vreal sector. Care little for her acquired family as she did, Plaxis was still the company her parents had founded. The only daughter of their union made certain to stay abreast of all public information.

Scotia's overly-freckled nose wrinkled. "I'm terrible with faces. I wish I had your sharp memory."

"No, you don't. It's a blessing to be able to forget things easily."

The awkward level inched up as Scotia rode out the subtext. In their silence, they refocused on the tail end of Johanna's speech.

"...and I know you'll all join me now in officially congratulating Miss Fife on her new position."

A polite round of applause, short lived, tapered off. The lobby began to empty, each of the workgroups flowing towards their area of the tower. Cindira knew she needed to get back to her workstation in the Kitchens—a new batch of specialization orders had come in and she'd be coding till doomsday—but something about the way the curious man lingered forced her to do the same. She'd stay until she couldn't avoid being noticed.

"Cindira?"

She gave Scotia's elbow a little tap. "You, um... go on ahead. I should step forward and pledge my fealty to the new queen or something. Johanna will tell my dad I was acting *unappreciative* and *unsupportive* if I don't say something to Kaylie in front of everyone, especially since she just officially became my boss."

"You know what I think of that, right?"

It was a rhetorical question, of course. Or at the very least, it was one Scotia was getting tired of answering on Cindira's behalf.

Finally, the redhead shrugged. "Whatever, you're a big girl. I, however, do have to go." Scotia leaned in closer to Cindira's ear under the guise of trying to hug her friend. "In prison, this would be where I shove the shank into your pocket so you could take care of her."

"Love you, too."

Luckily, Kaylie's inner fandom, a hobnobbed collection of sycophantic residue feeding off each other's counterfeit glee, flanked the rising star, giving Cindira a shield of invisibility as she crept up to the edge of the gaggle.

"Oh, Kaylie!" One of them squealed, positively shaking with glee as she presented a hand. "Director of Code Integrity and Specialization! That's where all the elites go when they want VIP treatment and code. You're going to be the go-to person for kings, actors, CEOs... Everyone who's anyone in the Kingdom. What an honor."

"It is, isn't it?" was her stepsister's snide, curt reply. The soft-skinned hand drew back as soon as it could be done without looking like a snap. For a moment, Kaylie's eyes met Cindira's. A wicked smile peeled across her face. "Say, mother, isn't my new position the one that Omala Grover once held?"

Johanna's hands clawed her daughter's shoulders as she snaked her arms around her. "Don't be silly, dear. I have Omala's old position."

As she was both the Executive Vice-President of Plaxis, and Rex Tieg's wife, Cindira couldn't be sure which Johanna was talking about. Neither sat well.

Cade whittled himself from the crowd, pushing forward to get to his sister's side. Kaylie's twin was gray where she was bright, almost as if he'd grown pale living in her shadow. Cindira remembered having that thought the first time they'd met as children, in a time when she'd give herself over to fantasy and poetry about the wonders of the world. Kaylie was the sun, and Cade, silver moonlight. Hauntingly handsome in his own way but given to silence and sulking. Cindira had once pictured the twins in the womb looking like some sort of infantile yin-yang. He'd never been as hostile to her as the two women had, but there was a bit of sinister in his silence. Cindira suspected his motives–especially as she'd grown into womanhood. Forget the fact that they'd been stepsiblings since she was nine and he, fifteen. Much worse went on inside the Kingdom, she'd heard.

He paused on the outer orbits when he saw her, smiling and laying a hand on her shoulder. "Cindy."

"Cade."

A world lay between what she wished she could say and what her tongue would agree to. *Did you see me last night? What were you doing there? Were you spying? For my father, or your mother?* But this was hardly the place to discuss such things.

Luckily, Cade filled the hallow spaces between them, veering off into an appearance of polite conversation. "I thought I saw that friend of yours here." He looked around. "What was her name again?

"Scotia." As she'd told him the last two times he asked. "And I don't think she's your type."

His smug smile faltered at the veiled jab. "You don't know that."

Cindira grimaced. "True, she might have a thing for reptiles I'm not aware of."

"If I were a snake, Cindy, you'd be the first one I'd bite."

"Would you like to see what it's like?" She stepped forward, curving into him so only he could hear her words. "I could do it, you know: code a snake over someone's avatar. Then, I could find it, pin it down, and chop off its head."

Cade winced. "But you never jack into any of our platforms."

"Not since my mother died, no. But if someone was trying to do something, let's say *questionable* with a good friend of mine, I might."

Her stepbrother's eyes widened. "There's no way you'd ever get away with it. It would kill me in the real if you chopped off my head there."

"Thanks to those security precautions your mother insisted on. But if I only recoded a very *specific* part of your avatar..." Her eyes flashed down to his pants suggestively. "The Kingdom is a powerful platform, and I've spent the last three years slaving, learning how to manipulate every, single part of it."

Plaxis's creation demanded sacrifice. Long days, longer nights, all at the cost of a significant personal life. For Cindira, anyhow. The Fife twins always found time for parties, vacations, and romance. Meanwhile, membership to the Kingdom was prohibitive; only the uber wealthy could afford such a thing. But once inside the world's must exclusive vreal, the only way to stand out was customization. Of avatars, of dresses, of homes, of... certain physical abilities. Each required a herculean amount of coding. Since joining the Kitchen staff, Cindira's designs and modification had earned her a demanding audience, even if no one outside the staff knew who the mystery designer was. Kaylie, as a VIP liaison, made sure of that. Since Cindira wanted to remain out of the public eye, she let her. But that didn't change the truth.

Her personal life now was confined to one night a week. A good thing, too. Kaylie and Johanna still had no idea how many hours

Cindira had logged in secretly, patching up the weakening source code with whatever programming bandages she could manage. She'd be damned if she saw either the Kingdom or Gaia go dark on her watch. She owed it to her mother's memory to make sure of it.

Perhaps drawn by her son's gravity, Johanna had made her way over without either noticing, appearing suddenly at their backs. "Slaving is such a strong word, Cindira, and it isn't as if you haven't been well compensated."

"Indeed." Cindira shifted gears, driving away from the fact that Plaxis's success had come on the back of her mother's legacy. "I was going to say congratulations to Kaylie, but I don't think her fan club will let me."

"Yes, well, it can be difficult to get the attention of powerful people."

Johanna wrapped an arm around Cindira, pulling her into the fold. Family intimacy was served only for the eager eyes about them. Employee morale had been suffering before Cindira's arrival, and the illusion of a big, happy family leading the company proved a successful cure. Besides, Johanna wasn't about to miss a chance for her stepdaughter to genuflect at the feet of her own flesh and blood.

"Kaylie? Come over here." Johanna called. Then, turning back to Cindira, she grinned. "Demands are met. Requests are only *considered*. Remember that, will you?"

"Ah-hmm..."

All blinked in surprise at the sound of someone clearing his throat, though Johanna regained her composure the fastest. Cindira managed to shuffle behind Johanna as they turned, but she could still see the particulars. It was him, the man that she and Scotia had noticed. He stood on the edge of their small gathering, his eyes intent but his body retracted, as though asking for permission to join them while daring any of them to deny the request. Up close, Cindira could see a scarred line through his right eyebrow and the slight curvature of his nose that might be a healed injury of another sort. He became aware of her just as her gaze drifted to his gray eyes. The man looked at her in a cold and analytical way. Without reason, she began to feel like she was guilty of something. The message was communicated without words: he didn't want her there. He wanted either Johanna or Kaylie's attention. Maybe both.

When Johanna acquiesced and didn't bite back with one of her typical belittling or dismissive comments, Cindira took the opportunity to melt back just enough to still remain within earshot. Her interest was piqued now. Who was the man, and why was Johanna treating him like someone important? He couldn't be a client; far too formal and somber. Not a supplier or a vendor; there's no way anyone with such a menial role in her stepmother's assessment would be invited to this area of the building. Cindira looked down at the comque on her wrist, trying to appear consumed with it. Streaming out a steady drip of information on news, weather, gossip, messages, even biometrics, the little ubiquitous devices always had something to offer when she was trying to avoid engaging with others.

"Officer Batista." Johanna pulled a tissue smile onto her face, a countenance utilitarian and quickly disposed of when finished. "May I introduce you to my family?"

Cindira's stomach bottomed out as Johanna said "My daughter..."

A moment later, Kaylie bounced into view, back ever so slightly arched to enhance the view of her bosom. Curiouser and curiouser. Did she know who the stranger was? One might think so, the way she deployed her typical tricks designed to subvert a man's clear thinking in response. Then again, maybe that was Kaylie being Kaylie. After all, *Officer Batista* wasn't unkind to the female eye.

"And my son, Cade."

Cade trod forward, offering the officer a hand and quick nod of recognition. Meanwhile, Cindira waited to see if she would be acknowledged. When she wasn't, it came more as a relief than a surprise. She should take this opportunity to turn on heel and flee, but then the man spoke, and her feet refused to move.

"Thank you for allowing me to visit today. It's such an honor to see where Omala Grover made history."

His voice arrested her. She'd heard it before... somewhere? The scent of memories drifted on the breeze and shooed away. *Cedar and myrtle and wild animals, and the sound of men shouting...* So much for the perfect memory all her fellow code writers credited her with. This man's voice triggered a tripwire of recollection, an explosion of the past that refused to gain clarity in the lifting smoke.

It couldn't just be his accent. Yes, she had heard that, even though he'd been well instructed in English to minimize it. South American maybe? No, European. He'd said *thank you*, not *tank you*. Spanish or Portuguese? Oh, it was going to drive her crazy. She knew him, but how?

"Kaylie?" Johanna's tenuous mezzo brought Cindira back to the moment. "I promised Officer Batista a tour of the Kitchens. Perhaps you'd be willing to show him around?"

"Of course. It would be my *pleasure.*"

Kaylie put a lilt in her voice that imbued every word with a hint of innuendo. Was there a mission decreed by her mother, or did she just want to bed Batista on the merits of his own physical appeal? At least there, Cindira couldn't blame her. Batista was handsome. Naturally, which made him even more attractive, for some reason. But Authority personnel were a dime a dozen. Why would Johanna pull Kaylie from her tool chest for a lowly officer? Kaylie was used to managing senators, regulators, criminal investigators.... Or was this man something more than just a run-of-the-mill Authority?

Officer Batista grinned. "That's where Omala Grover once worked, isn't it?"

Cindira didn't need to see her stepmother's face to know she was scowling. Johanna detested when someone mentioned Omala in her company, but she'd never downplay the truth. "Omala *was* the Kitchens," she said. "She invented the programming language that powers our source code and built the initial frameworks for Gaia. The Kingdom, architecturally speaking, is its duplicate. But no, Omala never worked in this building. The original Gaia Labs were located across town in the Old Mint."

The officer shoved his hands into his pockets. "Really? That's too bad. I'd love to see where the source code was first developed. Where the world was saved from the brink of destruction."

"Hyperbole doesn't suit you," Johanna laughed. "All Omala did was build the stage where the players could act."

Batista, while grinning, shook his head. "She did much more than that. Since the time my father was a member of the first Congress, it's been a place where men and women can work out their differences through either diplomacy or warfare, without the horrific real-world consequences. The thought of countries still going to war —*actual* war— chills me. The destroyed infrastructure, the damage to our planet, the needless loss of human life..." Batista looked down as if to compose himself. His focus drifted from the women to an antique watch on his wrist. "If not for Gaia, how much more would we have lost?"

Something shifted in the air, and suddenly, Johanna's sacrificial lamb needed to be pushed toward the knife more insistently. "Officer Batista—"

His attention snapped back. Batista wore a sober and, if Cindira hadn't known better, condescending shadow in his expression. "Let's stick with *Detective*, if you don't mind."

A detective? Even Cindira's own protective instincts flared at that notion, especially given the fact that he'd specifically mentioned the source code. Raising any concern would only cause more problems and draw Johanna's ire, however.

"Apologies, *Detective*." Johanna bowed her head. "If you wanted an overview of Plaxis's underlying architecture, it might be more effective to discuss that in Kaylie's office. The Kitchen is nothing more than a roomful of computer stations and code writers, none of whom are particularly good conversationalists."

"No, I'm very intent on seeing them." His smile was the kind where the corners of the mouth draw back instead of up. "It's the whole reason I'm here, if you'll remember."

Johanna went pale. The reaction could only be seen around the parts of her face not touched by the surgeon's tools, but after years spent reading them for any sign of crimson, Cindira knew where to look.

Who was this man, to have that sort of effect on this industry colossus?

Tucking her chin into her chest, Johanna demurred. "Of course, Detective. Kaylie, could you?"

"Oh, I'm more than happy to give the detective a peak of the Kitchens." Kaylie drew her arm through the air, motioning to the elevators, even as Cindira studied the flinch of Johanna's face. "After all, the place where we cook up all the code is really the heart of the company."

Batista cleared his throat and mimicked Kaylie's gesture, hooking his arm to hers. "Let's to it, then, Miss Fife."

"To the elevators. We have to go down to the nineteenth floor." To say Kaylie looked like a fisherman dangling a big catch as she walked by would be underselling the arrogance. Who was this man that she felt like she had to lord the fact they were so close over her fangirls? Was it just because he was someone she hadn't yet slept with? "If you'd like to follow me, I can—"

Kaylie's words cut out as a shriek flew from her mouth. Cindira spun just in time to see Detective Batista push her stepsister behind him, his arms akimbo, as a member of Kaylie's lingering retinue also cried out. Everyone else wheeled about then, setting their eyes on the hooked nose woman of small stature and large bosoms cowered behind a potted plant.

Johanna swooped in, clicking both heels and her fingers. "Really, Daria, what was that for?"

Perhaps *Daria* had begun to understand the comedy of her over-reaction as she squeaked out, "A mouse just ran out of the elevator."

Cindira, who found herself two feet closer to her stepsister than she'd been a few moments before, drew back, both literally and figuratively. A mouse wasn't any kind of threat. Not that she knew what she would have done if it was. Sometimes she forgot that out here in the real, she couldn't conjure weapons and make walls disappear.

If she could, Plaxis would be run a lot differently.

Still... a mouse way up here on the twenty-third floor? How did that happen?

Batista grinned as his stance relaxed. He again offered up his arm to Kaylie. "Don't worry, Miss Fife. I'm trained in many forms of defense. I'm sure one of them works on rodents."

THREE

CINDIRA ARRIVED IN the Kitchens and took shelter at her work-station, glad to see Kaylie and the detective had yet to arrive. It was a calculated risk, taking the stairs. Luckily it had paid off. Whereas she'd had a straight shot down four flights without interruption, the elevator had to pause to let each person out on a different floor as it came down.

Jeffrey Mackey—*Mack*, as everyone called him—didn't look up from his work as she busily brought up her command screens. "And how was the coronation?"

"Full of pomp and circumstance. I think there may have been cake too, but I didn't go looking." She populated one of her screens with the list of modification requests. Those would keep her working well into the night. "She's on her way here for her victory tour."

Mack leaned back in his chair, threading his hands behind his head while planking in place. "Should I get my lipstick on? Will I be expected to kiss ass?"

"More like kiss the ring." She pushed a finger against the first file in her queue. "She has some Authority pin with her, and they should be here... any...."

She saw a dozen sets of eyes perk up from behind each bank of monitors when the detective stepped off the elevator. It reminded her of animals who froze when a predator came into their midst. In a moment, the underlying soundtrack that characterized the Kitchens—styli skidding over screens, keyboards tapping, modulation kits clicking together—deadened to a hush. SF Authority had that effect wherever they went, but in a room where every coder by design sat in a circle and could easily exchange glances with the others, the awareness of the communal experience intensified the phenomena.

"There's no need for that." Kaylie waved a hand through the air.

"Just because I'm now the supervisor of this department doesn't mean you need to do anything differently or pause to hear commands just because I walk into the room. You can go on with whatever work you were doing before we came in."

Behind her monitor, Cindira rolled her eyes. *Leave it up to Kaylie to think that* she *was the one we were fixated on.* Slowly, then a little more with each second, the customary sounds started up again. Through a finger-wide gap between two of her monitors, the coder observed Kaylie and the detective step to the center of the room, where a cylindrical enclosure about a meter in diameter ran from floor to ceiling, serving as a Kitchens' central feature.

"What is this, some kind of escape chute?" Batista asked.

Kaylie huffed a laugh. "Hardly. It's a specialized interface that gives our coders a limited ability to manipulate a Plaxis vreal platform in real time. Officially, it's called the Interactive Lux Replicator Engine, but everyone here just calls it the Sink."

A corner of the detective's mouth twitched. "As in, the kitchen sink?"

"Coders are geeks." Her stepsister shrugged. "They like puns."

And they have ears and are the reason your family are insanely rich. Cindira kept the thought silent. Not *our* family. While she'd never claim she was poor, most of the inheritance from her mother had gone to pay for Cindira's schooling. Omala, it had turned out, donated the lion's share of her estate to charity. In any event, the wealth the Tiegs normally flaunted in public was something she had no share of, nor any desire to possess.

Batista's eyes narrowed. He gave Kaylie a diagnosing appraisal. "Do you always talk about your employees so flippantly right in front of them?"

Cindira buried her face into her chest. *Thank you, Detective.*

But her stepsister wasn't without her strengths. Kaylie was rarely taken aback, and when she was, she rebounded with haste.

"Speaking of our coders," Kaylie continued, flipping out a hand in Mack's direction, "this is where they work. A dozen stations, all of them with identical equipment: a keyboard, a box of prototyping supplies, a mishmash of personal effects. Here they can develop new code or tweak something that already exists, bring it up in the

Sink if they want to experiment or test things like luminescence or fluid dynamics, and dispatch any completed project into the user's vreal residence or village collection spot."

"And are these the same coders who maintain the source code?"

Any amusement in Kaylie's eyes fell away. "It maintains itself. Omala Grover designed it to be self-sustaining."

Batista rubbed the tip of his nose with his index finger. "Is that a no, then?"

"I'm sorry, it's not really something I can comment on further than that."

In a hurried rotation, Batista's eyes made a full round of the room, locking eyes with each coder in turn. When he got to Cindira, she turned to her screens, even as her cheeks heated. Hopefully her light olive skin masked it, though she could have sworn his eyes stayed on her a little longer than the others. What was he doing, Cindira wondered, looking for evidence that someone might crack and say what Kaylie wouldn't? Well, that wasn't going to happen, because no one *knew* anything else. Except for Cindira, of course, and she wasn't about to tell some handsome but unwelcome Authority that she'd been secretly and covertly keeping up the weakening source code for years.

When he seemed satisfied that there was nothing anyone else could offer on that particular thread, the detective pressed on. "Keyboards? No aural interfaces?"

The cadence of keying slowed from a fierce squall to a gentle passing shower. Mack caught Cindira's eye, pointing while he mouthed the words, *what's this guy after?* Cindira shrugged and opened up a DM interface on her workstation. Before she could send her best guess, Kaylie closed in on Mack's station for whatever show-and-tell she had planned.

"Pele, our AI assistant, is always on standby, but believe it or not, the code writers prefer the mechanical." Kaylie paused, leading the detective around to view Mack's workspace, pointing to the left-hand display filled with symbols, letters, and numbers. "Aural interfaces require natural speech. The Kingdom's supplemental code is all written in Purusha+. The code writers say it's quicker."

Mack's hands froze over the keyboard, the stream of key strikes ceasing with an audience watching. "It *is* quicker. Besides, can you imagine how loud this room would be if we were all simultaneously spouting code?" Suddenly, his hands went to his screen, spreading his fingers out wide to block as much of the view as possible. "I'm sorry, but this is a user's private information. It's not open for external review. Not unless you have a warrant."

Batista grimaced. This was a man who wasn't used to being told no and hadn't had a lot of opportunity in letting it go when he couldn't. As though the detective realized others might be reading his social cues, he unbuttoned his jacket and cleared his throat before resuming a nonchalant attitude.

"It wasn't my intention to pry. My apologies." He turned back to Kaylie. "Purusha+?"

"It's the language Omala Grover invented that Gaia is built on."

At the mention of her mother's name, Cindira perked up. She almost stood. *Almost.*

"I know what Purusha is," the detective continued, "but I thought it was something only its creator knew."

Kaylie led the way to the outer edge of the room, backing against one of the walls and arching her chest out in such a subtle way. Was she trying to distract Batista?

"I know that's what everyone says, but it's not entirely true," Kaylie said. "We've been able to ferret out enough of the language through the years to keep both the Kingdom and Gaia going. Grover might have thought she was doing something no one else was capable of, but we estimate we've been able to recover about eighty percent of it. Purusha+ is more of a derivative, really. No one will ever be able to do all that she could, but we're able to do all that she *did*."

"A gap of twenty percent of a language sounds pretty significant, Miss Fife." He turned his intense scrutiny on the coders with a slow sweep of his head. Cindira took eyes to her screen in desperation to remain invisible. "No one knows it all? Are you sure about that?"

"Yes." Her eyes narrowed. "Exactly what is it that you're investigating, Detective?"

Batista hesitated, his eyes filled with equations meant to measure Kaylie. Finally, he gave one miniscule nod and continued. "I'm here representing Gaia Security. I'm afraid that's all I'm at liberty to discuss."

Gaia security? Cindira's fingers went to her throat, stroking a thumb over the indent in flesh.

Her stepsister rolled her eyes toward the ceiling, gently swaying back and forth. "Sorry, I thought security officers were permajacked into Gaia?"

"*You* must know that's just a rumor. If we stayed permajacked, our bodies would atrophy, like a chiphead's." He held out his arms, inviting her to inspect his person as evidence. "As you can see, I'm not in any kind of diminished state."

No, he is not.

Kaylie acquiesced. "Fair enough. Dealing with Gaia wasn't part of my old job, but I'll have to come up to speed on it now. In this new position, I'm also the official liaison to the sovereign's office. Maybe you can help me by telling me why Gaia would want to know about the architecture of the Kingdom?"

Any trace of gaiety drained from his features as he held up a hand and traced a finger down the wall, drawing an invisible line that used the contours of Kaylie's body as a guide. "Miss Fife, have you noticed any subtle changes inside the Kingdom environment that you've found difficult to explain lately?"

"That's difficult to answer, Detective. It's constantly changing. The fashions, the color palates, the clientele. It might be a vreal based on a romanticized recreation of baroque opulence, but we still have to keep its visual appeal tracking in parallel to contemporary twenty-second century tastes."

The detective began to read fluently in Kaylie's language. He leaned in, flattening his hand against the wall, just right of her forehead. Cindira should have been used to the way that men threw themselves at her stepsister. Not that Kaylie made herself a difficult catch as long as the man pursuing had the body, money, connection, status, power, and/or secrets to make him worth her time.

Cindira grabbed her mug, faking a need to top off her coffee, to position herself close enough to hear as their voices softened.

"Rumor is, most of those fashions change because of the styles *you* yourself debut." He traced a finger over Kaylie's bottom lip. "You're quite the trendsetter, aren't you? But where do you get all your personal things designed? I hear that no one can code their equal."

"I'm afraid I don't share that information. If everyone knew who my designer was, she'd jack her prices sky high and never have time for me."

Rolling her eyes wasn't a choice, it was a form of therapy. Cindira bit the inside of her mouth. *Jack her prices up.* Had Kaylie ever paid Cindira a single credit for the hundreds of hours of labor she'd done? No. The reward, she'd said, was in building a portfolio. The mystery of the unknown designer would only add to intrigue, and one day, when Kaylie was ready to share her, she would. Three years of promises had built up quite a debt, one which Kaylie was in danger of defaulting on.

Batista leaned in, his lips inches from Kaylie's. It wasn't just Cindira gawking now. Not a single keystroke or mouse click could be heard.

"Can I at least see underneath?" He closed his eyes, as though he meant to kiss her, but didn't actually move a single bit. "Let me see the code?"

Though the two lust birds remained unaware, everyone else in the room turned on Cindira as she slammed her mug on the table next to the coffee pot. *Hell. No.* She'd be damned if anyone was going to peek at her code. Not even Kaylie was allowed to see, not that she'd expressed any interest. Cindira hadn't spent years fighting off hackers for some hot lips Gaia detective to swoop in and steal her designs.

Luckily, Kaylie backed her up for once—

"I'm sorry, but without a warrant or a direct order from my father..."

—even if she did so while claiming Cindira's dad as her own.

"...no one is allowed to see *any* code. Even the coders in this room have to grant each other permission to see each other's work."

Just as Kaylie got tired of waiting and leaned in, Batista swiveled, pulling away. The indifference had crept back into his voice. "The Kingdom has expanded since Omala Grover died fifteen years ago. In fact, she was found floating in the Bay the day after its public launch. How can you keep building if you don't have the full code set?"

Kaylie blinked away the confusion. "What we do here is mostly cosmetic," the blonde said plainly. "We can create buildings, design avatars—that kind of stuff. But we can't figure out how the wind blows or why gravity still is present. Did you know that every snowflake that falls in the Kingdom or Gaia is unique? The code that actually lets the Kingdom function is restricted."

"Restricted from whom?"

"Restricted from everyone."

Cindira couldn't stop the half-grin that blossomed onto her face. *Not everyone.*

Kaylie continued, "The Kingdom's source code was directly copied from Gaia, and since Gaia's source code was also only accessible by Omala Grover..."

The detective balanced his chin on his balled-up hand. "Are you telling me that even Plaxis doesn't know how the Kingdom works?"

"No one has ever known. Except Omala Grover, and the dead don't talk."

He stepped forward. "If you were called in front of the Gaia Congress and its High Court, could you testify to that under oath?"

The High Court only dealt with the most extreme international crimes. What in the hell was going on inside a hedonistic and frivolous world like the Kingdom that was being investigated with the same intensity as a war crime?

Kaylie swallowed. "Are you threatening me, Detective?"

"Not you." Batista reached up, vanity beaming from his smug smile. "Thank you for the tour, Miss Fife. It was very illuminating."

FOUR

FOG, AS WELCOME AS it was rare, cloaked Cindira's weary sojourn home. On nights like these, when the Kitchens kept baking code until after dark in response to some high roller's request, she longed most for the home she once shared with her mother. It still peeved Cindira that she hadn't been allowed to stay. *Can't happen,* her father had said a few days after the funeral when she'd suggested her nanny would be happy to live with her in the Nob Hill penthouse. *You just lost your mom, kiddo. I know it hurts to leave, but you need to be with family. An eleven-year-old can't live without a parent, and a nanny isn't really a parent.*

A thought she almost found comforting, to think her dad might finally step up and be more than a passing acquaintance. And for a little while, he was. Until the next fall when she was shipped off to boarding school. By then, however, it seemed the lesser of two evils. Kaylie and Cade vacillated between indifference and intolerance where she was concerned. With the five-year age difference, the older twins saw her as nothing but a little kid who had nothing to do with their lives and social circles. Johanna in the meantime barely acknowledged Cindira's presence, other than to occasionally reference her in the background of a conversation, during which she was customarily labelled either "Rex's kid" or "*that* woman's child." Exceptions proved the rule, and on the rare occasion when her parentage wowed a guest, she was forced to doll up and parade through the room as "the great Omala Grover's daughter." Johanna fawned with faux pride and sympathy, as though she were a saint who'd adopted an orphaned princess.

Cindira paused at the entry to her father's home—or, more appropriately, to the path that led to the guesthouse in the backyard—taking off her ventilator and stuffing it into her bag. City air had been predicted to clear up enough for long-term exposure two years ago. When the fog locked in the pollutants of the day, however, it was still a good idea to switch to filtered. If it weren't for Gaia, the ventilator might be a permanent necessity.

As her eyes tracked up from her side bag, a flash of white scurried across her path, making Cindira jump back and muffle a shout. Her hands tightened into fists as she chided herself. "Damn it, Cindira, it's a mouse, not a python."

Not that she'd care to run into one of those, either.

The gate protested with an eerie *creeeaaak*. Beyond it, an elderly woman with a mop of gray hair floating atop a nightshirt wielded a rake.

"Stop or else."

Cindira let the gate close behind her before crossing her arms over her chest. "Or else what, Auntie?"

"Auntie?" The gardening tool lowered as another arm came up to sweep away a hairline and expose the wrinkle-wrecked face of Asla Duncan. "Oh, Cindira! Cindira dear! I'm sorry. I just thought... I—"

"You were defending the house against thieves, thugs, and possibly, thespians. Yes, I know." Cindira dropped her bag at her side and divested her one-time nanny of the rake, setting it aside. "But as you can see, it's just me, as usual. You know that no one else comes in the back gate but the two of us."

Asla's eyes fluttered. "Not true. There was someone poking around back here this afternoon when I came in from my shift in the main house."

Cindira took up her bag. "Did you draw blood?"

"Ah! You make jokes. You never see the danger coming."

Cindira hooked her arm in the old woman's and walked her toward the front door, glad to have survived the impressive ninja broom skills. Ever since the night when Omala Grover had died, the former nanny saw monsters everywhere. For fifteen years, every doctor was a conspirator, every driver an assassin. She refused to accept the truth; Omala's death was nothing more than a tragic accident. Cindira's mother had slipped off the dock on a foggy, damp night and was hit by the very boat coming to pick her up. It could happen to anyone. It *had* happened to Omala.

Cindira decided to focus Asla's attention to the remaining question. "So who was it then?"

"Who was—Oh, some sort of delivery. A box with your name on it. I didn't open it."

"Did the package have a return address?"

"No, it wasn't post. Is there even post anymore? A courier from Plaxis came. I thought he meant to bring it to the main house for the family, but he swore it was for you."

"Why would Plaxis go to the expense of sending something here, when they could just drop it to me at the office?"

"He didn't say. Just a quick 'Is this where Cindira Tieg lives?' and that was it."

The guesthouse Cindira shared with the aging woman had originally been built as a pool house, a hundred years before. During the worst of the droughts that had come when Cindira was a baby, outdoor pools up and down the west coast were outlawed and forcibly filled. Only the outline of the former feature remained, creating a buffer between them and the main house. Now that Asla had been assured that it was only Cindira at the gate and not a thespian, she shuffled off to bed, leaving the younger woman alone with some reheated chapati, some shepherd's pie, and a box without an obvious way to open it.

As she turned it over in her hands, rotating it, looking for a seam, Cindira's imagination took off. Could it be a cake? A firesafe with a trove of money? A human head? Hopefully not that last one, though honestly, she wouldn't be interested in finding a head of *any* kind. Curiosity burned, even as reality frustrated. There was no keyhole or crease, but it wasn't empty. Every time the axis changed something moved within.

She'd have to follow up in the morning with the office, figure out who had dispatched the cube to her home, and why. For the moment, she wanted nothing more than a hot shower and cool drink—

Knock, knock, knock.

—Which would have to wait.

Kaylie was a woman born both annoyed and annoying. The moment Cindira opened the door, she plowed past and spun around, fists on hips. Why Asla didn't front evil-step-siblings-turned-bosses with broomstick in hand, Cindira couldn't say.

"I need a new dress."

"Please, make yourself at home," Cindira deadpanned, closing the door behind her stepsister.

A shaky voice called from behind a closed door. "Is it a thespian, dear?"

"No, Ms. Asla, it's only me, Kaylie," Kaylie called out over Cindira's shoulder before adding under her breath, *"crazy old bat."*

Cindira closed her eyes and huffed her frustration. She'd lecture—again—about respecting the elderly, if she thought it would do any good. At least Kaylie rarely said anything rude directly to Asla's face. What Cindira wouldn't give for the same consideration.

"Kaylie, I just got home. *Just.* And as I've told you ten times before, I can't design something that complex from here. Security protocols won't let me—"

The blonde interrupted, "I know, tap into the network from a location outside of HQ or an approved satellite office. But you don't understand. I *need* it. There's a ball tonight, and I just found out Maeve Connor copied the last design you made —by the way, what the hell? Don't you have my designs copyrighted?— and is wearing it *specifically* to make me look foolish."

Not sure she needs to go to such lengths. "I *do* have your designs—" *My designs.* "—registered, but that doesn't stop someone from making a pretty close knockoff. You know that. And I was just about to—"

"Hold on a second." Kaylie's hand traced an ominous arc, pointing to the table. "What. Is. *That.*"

Cindira didn't have a chance to conjure fresh annoyance at being interrupted yet again. Instead, she followed her stepsister's eyes, to where the mysterious box had been left for later inspection.

"That? It's nothing." Cindira's head quirked to the side as she took in the baffling sight. Not only had the box magically grown a lid; it was open.

"I know what *that* is." Kaylie managed to cross the room before Cindira could create an excuse to call her off.

"You do?"

"Yes, only... What the hell? Cindy, what are these?"

As Kaylie reached into the box and pulled out the contents, Cindira found herself asking the same question. At first glance, it appeared to be some sort of elongated dish or figurine. Whatever it was, it was mostly transparent. Only by relaxing her eyes and *not* focusing on it did Cindira come to understand the object balanced on the end of Kaylie's finger was a shoe.

A *glass* shoe.

Her stepsister laughed. "Somebody sure punked you good."

"They did?"

"Yes, they did."

One corner of Kaylie's mouth rose in a lopsided smirk. She palmed the shoe for just a moment before tossing it across the room. Cindira shifted – managing to snatch it from a certain cracked fate – and landed on the couch with her hair lashed across her face. But then, she discovered the effort was unnecessary. The shoe wasn't *glass*, per se. It was silicone. It had been molded to look like a ballet slipper and held that form well. Yet, there was a certain amount of give to it, like it could wrap around any foot, no matter the wearer. More of a footie, really, than a shoe.

"These are *supposed* to be a pair of Pris Leons, but they're counterfeit."

Cindira blew a raspberry. "Why would someone send me designer shoes and such ugly and absurd ones at that?"

She might be able to wear these under another pair of shoes and get by, but there was no way she'd feel safe walking down the littered streets of San Francisco and risk a puncture. Product design wasn't Cindira's specialty, but it didn't take a genius to figure out how foolish that would be.

Kaylie's face dropped. "Of course, I don't know. They'd certainly be wasted on you if they were real."

Apparently, her stepsister didn't think the design was impractical. No doubt she had three pair in her room in the main house at this very minute. Kaylie picked up the box, turning it and looking inside. A *swish-swash-swish* suggested the other shoe lay within, but the soured look on Kaylie's face also implied nothing else of interest did. Cindira suspected her stepsister had been hoping to find some kind of note explaining the parcel's purpose. Honestly,

Cindira wouldn't have minded learning that herself.

Finally, after a moment, Kaylie tossed the box back on the counter and moved on as if nothing else had happened. "Anyways, as I was saying: dress."

"I can't. I'd have to go back to Plaxis to—"

But Kaylie was already heading toward the door. "Don't forget, I'm your boss now. That can be a good thing, or a very bad thing for you."

"I could quit, you know." Cindira crossed her arms. "Lots of other places would love to have me. Tangentry would *love* it."

"And leave the company your parents built from the ground up? What would Omala say if she found out her only daughter went to work for the competition?" Kaylie paused to turn. "The dress: in my Kingdom closet ASAP. Don't forget shoes, necklaces, etc."

"Fine, but I can't design anything too complex from scratch *that* quickly. I'll modify one of the existing files."

"Whatever. Just make it different enough to piss off Maeve and teach her a lesson about trying to copy me."

FIVE

BY THE TIME CINDIRA arrived back at the office, only the night guards and a few people in the complimentary customer service suite were still in the building. The former knew Cindira on sight and didn't bother to ask why she was at work so late in the night; it wasn't Kaylie's first time being a diva. The latter were jacked into the vreal and weren't even aware of her existence as she passed by.

Cindira threw down her bag on her desk and called up the Kitchen's AI assistant.

Pele's soft feminine voice filled the space. "Good evening, Miss Tieg. How may I be of service?"

"I'm here by myself." *Again.* "I'm going to need help running the ops while I work inside the Sink. Open a portal into the Kingdom and take me to Kaylie's room."

More than just a sandbox when developing new elements for the vreal, Cindira had discovered the Sink's dual utility as a semi-jacked environment by accident on yet *another* night before yet *another* ball. One of the tangible-light diodes (TLDs) in the floor of the Sink needed to be replaced. Not able to wait until morning when the staff techanics would arrive, she'd decided to handle the matter herself. Cindira forgot, however, to turn the projectors off. The way her coworkers hailed her for discovering that everything inside and technically in the Kingdom responded to her touch in the vreal, she might as well have cured lunarity pox.

A low hum accompanied a scramble of colors inside the Sink as the power flicked on. Cindira crawled in through the service hatch and into the chamber, a small thrill running up her spine as the TLDs, embedded in the floor, ceiling, and walls fired up and beamed at her from all directions.

Pastoral landscapes whisked by, the image dodging people—other clients inside the environment—panning over cobble-stoned streets and around the VAPORs until, at last, it reached the front of her family's Kingdom residence, Alsace. Styled after a picture Kaylie had once seen of a baroque French chateau, the two-story brick home with narrow turrets on its left and right flanks looked out of place in the heart of the Kingdom's urban center, with its rows of grand townhouses pushing out from either side. Cindira knew Kaylie hadn't been happy about its "pitiful" scale. For once, Johanna had put her foot down on her own daughter's vanity for the most mundane of reasons: money. The profits to be made from the lots closest to the markets and the palace district were far too lucrative to waste on Kaylie's self-indulgence.

Pele's voice filtered through a speaker above. "Authorization required to enter the private residence of... Alsace. Please state passcode for user *Kitchen316* to enter the premises of *Her Majesty, Queen Johanna Tieg*."

Cindira's fingers flexed and tightened as a wave of disgust curdled her insides. "Minion."

The image dove forward again, through the front door, past the luxe entryway and the chandelier overhead, up the stairs, and into Kaylie's private suite. Once the image settled inside Kaylie's room and in front of her wardrobe, Cindira set about her work.

The microscopic sensors embedded in the glass around her read each movement, translating *real* world actions into *vreal* world manipulations. Though she knew there was no actual brass handle within her grasp, Cindira's mind created faux sensations suggesting otherwise. The wardrobe the length of a king-sized bed held gowns. Dozens of them in a rainbow of colors and a caravan of materials. Clients made certain agreements when they paid to play inside this virtual landscape, one being that, in order to maintain the esthetic of the fairytale world, they must dress appropriately. For women, this meant complex layers of petticoats, chemises and corsets – all designed and sold for a tidy profit by trendy designers. But even the most talented etailor that New York or Hong Kong had to offer couldn't do what Cindira could with code.

In short order, Cindira located one of the older dresses on file. A trail of chiffon and lace danced over the floor as she pulled it out. It was indeed one of her better creations. The secret to its appeal, the tiny twinkling diodes coded into the fabric that made it shimmer in even the dimmest light. Technically, the conception of such a thing would have been flagged by the team in charge of observing and maintaining the Kingdom's esthetic integrity. This was one instance where Kaylie being Kaylie helped Cindira push the boundaries. No one was going to flag something worn by a high-ranking Plaxis executive and the stepdaughter of Rex Tieg as non-compliant.

Cindira took a moment, studying the gown, conceptualizing its iterations.

"Pele, give me an interface up here."

"Acknowledged."

Like some sort of technical wisp-o-the-willows, a soft glow emerged, a floating tablet filled with numbers, letters, and genius. The code. Most saw only the rudimentary meaning behind the series of symbols, picking out the sections that served to express the augmented representation of each element of the dress floating in the air before her. Cindira saw form, shape, beauty. A few changes, including moving the color from green to yellow and shifting about the pleats and diodes, and the only thing remaining was to follow the template change with the accessories. After which, she hung her creation on the door of the closet, admiring it. It really was quite a gorgeous piece. Elegant, luxurious, yet simple in its form. Kaylie would turn every head in the palace when she entered wearing it. Cindira reached out, running her fingers over the fabric, imagining the sensation of silk on her palm was real.

"User approaching," Pele announced.

Kaylie must have jacked in early to check on Cindira's work. Which meant it was time to go. Not that her stepsister would see her if she came in. Though Cindira could interact with VAPORs in the Sink as if she were jacked in, she remained invisible to actual clients. She instinctually turned to witness the look in Kaylie's eyes when she saw the refashioned dress, the closest thing to appreciation she'd get, when a very unexpected thing happened.

It wasn't Kaylie. It wasn't even Cade or Johanna. Hell, it wasn't even her father, though after two months of the silent treatment, she'd actually welcome that for once.

Who did enter instead was Detective Batista.

"What are you doing here?"

He couldn't hear her. Cindira hadn't engaged the intercom that allowed someone in the Kitchens to be piped into the section of the Kingdom framed in the Sink. Otherwise, she'd do some *detecting* of her own. The Tieg vresidence had been set up with the strictest security protocols. Just because Batista was Authority and working on Gaia's behalf didn't give him the right. With a warrant, he could compel his way in, but there's no way Cindira wouldn't have heard about that. For reasons she didn't understand entirely, she found herself suddenly on the defensive for a family that in turn felt it owed her nothing.

"Leave," she commanded to dead air, before remembering she had her AI assistant at the ready. "Pele, remove the other user in this space. Move him, oh, let's say, fifty feet from the property boundary, two feet off the ground."

The fall he was about to experience wouldn't hurt him, but it would serve as a fair warning.

"Cannot comply."

Cindira bit her tongue, reminding herself it was illogical to get angry at something that lacked sentience. "And just *why* can you not comply?"

"You do not have the authority to override user."

"Doubtful, I have Class 1B clearance. The only people at Plaxis who can override me are my father and Johanna." Probably Kaylie now too that she was the boss. Hopefully Kaylie herself hadn't realized that yet. "Dad's not around, and there's no way Johanna let this guy in. She didn't even want to give him the time of day, let alone a self-guided tour of Alsace. *Remove him.*"

Two beeps, and then the same message. "Cannot comply."

What the... Cindira cocked her hip and scanned her thoughts for a solution. "What security clearance level does the other user in this space have?"

"User Batista has Full Administrative access to all systems."

Impossible. "On whose authority?"

"By the authority of Omala Grover."

Well, that definitely wasn't right. Cindira's shoulders fell, and she made a mental note once she was done with this errand to see if she could patch up the source code and this security gap. At the same time, she had her explanation. If Batista was working on Gaia's behalf, he might be some kind of hacker. Maybe he'd even found a way to piggyback on her entry. Whatever the case, he wasn't supposed to be here, and she wanted him gone.

Before Cindira could finish talking, the door to the bedroom opened. Vesuvius would admire the way her blood pressure blew up. The form of the condemnation coming her way took shape in her imagination: Kaylie was going to see Batista and point an immediate finger at Cindira's messy security code.

But as Cindira spun, shouting pointlessly to the detective to leave before he was seen, she discovered the officer had beaten her to the punch.

She was alone.

A smile stretched across Kaylie's face as she saw her remodeled dress hanging on the door of the wardrobe. Cindira's wayward relation walked right through her, oblivious to her presence, her arms held out to embrace the latest creation.

"Perfect!" Kaylie said. "Take that, Maeve. We'll see who Shapur goes home with tonight, won't we?"

As Kaylie began to strip off her Kingdom avatar's default wardrobe, Cindira couldn't get away fast enough.

SIX

"WHERE IN THE HELL AM I?"

Francisco was a man of habit. He liked regulation and schedule and discipline. Maybe that's what had drawn him to public service: it was a profession that both demanded and provided structure. That being said, when he clocked in to report to work as he did each night at 11pm San Francisco time, he was much aggrieved to discover that the jacking had failed to connect him correctly. Wherever his feet had landed in the vreal, this was most definitely *not* Gaia.

The house outside of which he stood wasn't large, but what it lacked in size it made up for with attention to detail. Long grass glistened in the morning sun (all Plaxis platforms operated in a Central European time zone). A row of tiny blue and yellow flowers lined a cobblestone walk to a front door made of wood and shaped like an archway. When he pushed, he found it open. Inside, luxurious furnishings, priceless pieces of art, and not a single modern amenity.

No electric lamps, no charge ports, no heating vents.

A fireplace crackled, a welcoming fire dancing on the hearth.

"I'm in the Kingdom." Francisco paused at the base of a staircase. "Pete? Pete, can you hear me?"

Maybe his operator back in the jackpod floor had already turned off their observation window. Every member of the staff knew that their boss liked privacy. If he were wise, Francisco would utter the set of words and make the necessary gestures to tell the AI embedded in the vreal that he needed assistance. People were waiting on him. He was an important man with appointments to keep. He didn't have time to sate curiosity for curiosity's sake.

And then he heard a groaning hinge as the door at the top of the stairs opened.

A chill shot down his back. His pulse quickened in anticipation of someone emerging and catching him in someplace he had no right to be. Which, he thought in hindsight, was ridiculous. Who was anybody on this platform to tell *him* he had no right to be there? He could go anywhere. After a few moments passed and no one emerged, however, the mystery of what lay above proved too tempting.

The bed chamber was organized chaos. A four-poster bed sat at the far end, next to a window with the view of distant, snow-capped mountains modeled after the Alps. While the bedding looked clean and sumptuous, it also lay in a haphazard pile in the middle of the mattress. Over the headboard and footboard, fabrics dyed in blues and greens had been left out to collect dust, though the beading and embroidery work suggested the coder who created them had done so with a great amount of attention to detail. It must have been as expensive as hell. The cost of real-world fashion could no longer hold a candle to some of the exuberant prices charged by the most in-demand coders.

Whoever lived here had no lack of funds to have so many dresses, or to treat them with such blatant disregard. True, in the vreal, cloth never spoiled and clothing could be cleaned with a simple command line. This, however, spoke of a certain type of personality who saw the works of someone's hard labor as things to be collected and disregarded without care.

Behind him, Francisco heard a noise. He spun, expecting to find he had been discovered at last. In those seconds, he prepared his opening line, a declaration of why whomever he found had no reason to demand him to leave. Only, there was no one there.

Not unless you included the little white mouse that ran along the floorboard.

Hmm, rodents in the Kingdom. It really is a hyperreality platform.

Then, another noise, this one almost like a woman's voice far in the distance. He looked around, trying to find a source. Maybe the voice was coming from the street outside? Only, the window was closed, as was the door downstairs.

And then, to add to his growing discomfort, Francisco had the sudden feeling that he was being watched.

No sooner had the thought registered, however, than the scene before him shifted. Walls, ceiling, floor, his body... They all froze then, just as quickly, began to defragment. Little pieces of his person were flying off into the distance. The sunlight faded.

He was back.

Pete through open the lid of the jackpod, his face red, his breath racing. "Are you okay, sir?"

Waking in the real was like stepping into a lukewarm shower. It stung for a moment, and then the body adjusted and relaxed. Francisco reached up as his vision equalized and his ears stopped ringing.

"What happened?"

"A failed launch." Pete looked back over his shoulder. No doubt the team of operators still at their stations were just as flustered as their director. "Your bios check out, but are you okay? Do you feel like you need medical attention?"

"Medical attention? No, I'm fine, I'm..."

He sat up and realized that, no indeed, he wasn't fine. He was back in the real.

And someone was *still* watching him.

SEVEN

THE GUY DID NOT EXIST.

Strictly speaking, Cindira knew that wasn't true. Of course, Detective Batista existed. She had seen him, watched him talk with Kaylie, found herself blushing when, for the slightest moment, their gazes had met. He had been real, but the story he'd conjured? Anything but.

Three nights of scrapping through public records after work, and nothing. She needed a break.

She shook the milk carton, relieved to find that there was just enough left for her tea. As much as people liked to joke she was her mother's copy, Cindira differed from Omala on that. Chai must be taken sweet and blond. "Like I like my men," Scotia had once quipped. The hot drink rushed down her throat, a liquid version of meditation that cleared her mind and set her at ease. Cindira crawled under her blanket and picked up the bifold datapad on her lap, determined to find out who in the hell this Batista character really was. More time only brought more frustration.

"How in this age does a person *not* exist online?"

Say what you might about the Authority and their strict, sometimes overreaching ways of keeping peace in the Pacific States, they were at least transparent when it came to their personnel. They *wanted* their people to be recognized, their power in part derived from the sense that they were omnipresent. Batista had no records in their database, or in the databases of any of the other tangential organizations the Authority occasionally outsourced to. Whatever trick he'd used, she wanted to know it. More concerning was why someone would *want* to hide who he really was. The list of motivations that populated her mind's eye made her shudder.

Maybe if she went to Plaxis and scoured the systems directly? Cindira deposited her teacup on the table next to her bed and shuddered again. Okay, so the guy wasn't who he said he was, but that didn't mean he wasn't a potential threat to the company somehow. Creating a trail tied to her employee login investigating his particulars might look like trying to dig up dirt to an outsider. Ironically, it was better to stick to the public places of the web.

She wracked her brain for every bit of information she could remember from her brief observation. Hadn't he said his father had been one of the early representatives to the first Gaia congress? She scoured records, cross-referencing the list of male members with those who also had sons working in the security forces. The few hits she got resulted in profiles that didn't match the interloper's appearance. Just to be fair, she repeated the process with the second and third congresses. Still no match. A fourth search turned up empty as well.

Her fingers hovered over the keyboard, poised but directionless. What else could she do? She'd taken Batista at his word, had no reason to suspect that the man Johanna Tieg referred to as a detective could be anything but.

Johanna. Cindira didn't credit her stepmother with very many positive traits, but one thing she would say of the second Mrs. Tieg was that she ran a tight ship. System integrity and security were paramount items of concern at Plaxis, both because the Kingdom's profitability demanded it, but more so because their clientele did. The affluent and the wealthy counted on the platform to be their private playground. Long gone were any innocent notions that participants in the vreal merely enjoyed the fairytale pageantry, even if that was the way it was marketed. While guidelines and liability considerations led to rules dictating the types of behavior clients could engage in "in public" while jacked in, behind closed virtual doors, anything and everything was game. How, then, had Johanna let an unknown entity into their midst?

Maybe she hadn't. Maybe Johanna was perfectly aware of who Batista really was.

He'd been interested in the architecture behind Plaxis's worlds, hadn't he? He'd been young, attractive, open to Kaylie's flirting, even one-upping her to a point that had Cindira herself envious. Batista did everything that was needed to get Kaylie to lower her defenses. Kaylie wasn't Johanna, and she'd let herself be played like an antique synthesizer.

But how did that connect with what she'd witnessed? How had Batista gotten into Kaylie's room? Even if he was Johanna's minion, there was no way Kaylie would have agreed to that intrusion. Not unless they had arranged a clandestine meeting, anyway. Given that the man had mysteriously disappeared the second Kaylie had shown up, that didn't seem likely.

Cindira threw down her pencil and took to her feet. Maybe the place to look for answers wasn't online, in the great big world, or in a database. Maybe the answers she sought were sitting in the big corner office at Plaxis.

She had to know. Not because she cared a lick about what went on in the Kingdom. Frankly, she didn't even really care if the platform disappeared tomorrow. But since it was a clone of Gaia, whatever threatened it, threatened her mother's true legacy as well. Johanna certainly wasn't about to go to bat for it.

Which left Cindira on deck.

EIGHT

JOHANNA TIEG HELD THE same opinion of rain that she did of her stepdaughter; it was a necessary inconvenience that ultimately did a lot of good if she could tolerate its occasional appearance.

Over the edge of her display, Cindira's hands crossed in front of her as she walked into the room. Johanna tapped the button on her headset so she could switch from dictation to manual keying and keep the tail end of the message she was writing private, pausing a moment to hold up one of her long, ringed fingers to request silence. Say what she would about Omala Grover, her predecessor in both the boardroom and the bedroom, at least she had raised Cindira to be compliant. She'd never admit aloud that her own children could have done with a bit more of that in their rearing, but then, she'd rarely admit it to herself either.

Finally, after she'd sent the message requesting an update of tomorrow's plans, she sat back, steepling her hands before her. "Is there something you need, Cindy?"

Cindira assumed a seat across the desk. "Since Kaylie is busy getting a handle of her new position, I thought I could be the one to tell you about the detective's visit to the Kitchens last week."

A lie. They both knew damned well that if Johanna had wanted to know, she would. Assuming she already didn't. Nevertheless, one did have to follow polite social norms until given a reason to do otherwise.

"Oh? Very well, then."

"He wanted to know about the architecture that underlays the Kingdom." Cindira's eyes narrowed almost imperceptibly. "Kaylie told him, as I've told you many times, that most of what makes it function was only known to my mother."

Another lie? Johanna wasn't sure, and it was that uncertainty that kept Cindira both employed and alive.

"Did he believe that?"

The girl's fingers curled around the arm of the chair in which she sat. "It's the truth."

"Of course, it is." Johanna let out a long breath through her nose, pushing herself back from her desk. "But that resurfaces our old, unsolved problem, doesn't it? We *need* to know how it all works. We can't just keep throwing code on top of code. Eventually, we're going to cross some tripwire or make everything too top-heavy, and it's all going to come crashing down. I wish you'd get over yourself and hack into it."

Cindira guffawed. "I'm good, but I'm not that good. I'm not... I'll never be able to do what my mother could."

Not likely. One of the reasons Johanna had hated Grover so much, was that she never lost appreciation for how talented she was. Even after Johanna had stolen Omala's husband and her company, she had no doubt that a woman as intelligent as her husband's ex-wife had planned for every contingency, including murder. For fifteen years, no one had questioned the events as presented on the night Omala had died. It was so foggy then, and the dock was slippery after years of neglect. And then there was the fact that Omala had worn that *stunning* blue sari with all its wrap-around layers and extra cloth. Once she slipped into the water, the poor thing must have become entangled in her own clothing. Oh, yes, Johanna was there; she'd walked Rex's ex to the docks. They *were* on amiable terms, after all? That had been documented by the gossip streams. But what was Johanna to do in the situation? She could barely see her own hands in front of her face, and she didn't know how to swim.

It seemed the perfect murder. There was no reason to believe anyone was the wiser. But what if there was evidence somewhere in the system? The things Grover could do, the things she was rumored to have done... There was a reason so many people referred to her as "Saint Omala." The woman worked miracles.

But at the end of the day, Johanna had a company to run, even with her inability to marvel the world in quite the same way.

"You leave me no choice, then. I'm going to have to hire outside hackers to get to the code for us."

Cindira's face screwed up. "Let all those underworld tech scum who are constantly launching attacks into our systems do it for pay?

They'd hold the source code for ransom the second they had it and sell it to the highest bidder, and it could never be secure again."

"Then I'd just have to make sure we're the top bidder." Johanna turned her eye back to her screen. "Anything else you'd like to discuss? I'm very busy today."

"No, just please, don't.... Don't hire those people." Cindira stood and made to leave, hesitating only a moment later, turning with a finger in the air. "Oh, there was one other thing the detective asked."

Johanna's eyes had already picked up where they'd left off on the message she'd been perusing. "Yes, what is it?"

"He asked Kaylie, if she was called in front of the Gaia Congress and its High Court, would she be able to swear under oath that the source code is unbroachable by anyone. *That* seemed a weird question for Authority to ask of us instead of the Royal Court's people talking directly to ours. Has something happened between Plaxis and Gaia that they feel the need to outsource now? Some kind of breakdown in communication?"

Johanna's pulse ticked in her forehead. Was Rex's shy and reserved daughter baiting her? Fine, if the child wanted to take a turn at the big girl's table, she would give her a sample of the service. "For your sake, you'd better hope so."

But the young woman failed to bend. In fact, Cindira seemed downright unflappable. "My suspicion is that Batista wasn't with Authority at all, but Gaia. Which makes me wonder, is he really acting on their behalf, or do they have a rogue agent? Maybe I should talk to my father about this?"

"He's not, and neither you nor I will disturb him with that fact. Your father's under a lot of pressure right now. Let him have his space."

"I haven't seen or spoken to him for two months now. How much more space should I give him?"

"As much as he needs. He'll let you know when he has time for a visit."

"Good. And please, remind him that I literally live in his backyard. Whenever he has a moment, I'm available. That's all."

Cindira turned towards the door, and had almost gotten to it, when

Johanna thought the better of it. "If you're on your way back down to the Kitchens, would you mind passing along a message? Please remind everyone who was there during Batista's visit last week that the NDAs each of you has signed forbids you from discussing anything that goes on inside that space *outside* of that space."

"Except for me, because Dad said I didn't have to sign one."

"That's right, he did, didn't he?" She brought her acidic glare into full view. "Which means, if I hear anyone's been asking around or performing in-house searches about who Batista really is, I'll know exactly which little codejockey was the culprit, won't I?"

For a moment, Johanna had feared that Cindira knew the truth. She didn't. But like her surly mother, the daughter's ability to seek without being sought was awe-inspiring. Best to remind her that what she saw as a strength, her father's minor bending of the rules where she was a concern, was also a liability.

"You know who he is."

Johanna said nothing. Instead, she stared fixedly, waiting. Finally, when Cindira saw the conversation was over whether she liked it or not, she turned and took her leave.

With that, Johanna deflated.

There was no point in the documents right now. She needed a few moments to collect herself. Shoulders sagging, Johanna pushed back from the desk and tapped her comque, accessing the part of the memory where the image she'd received two months ago was stored. She wasn't sure why she still kept it. She'd looked at it so often, the picture was burned into her mind, along with the message that had accompanied its receipt.

If you ever want to see him again, you know what to do.

Rex's tears were visible, even though the layers of security embedded in the files to keep it untraceable reduced its quality. His hands tied behind his back and blotchy bruises on his face, he appeared to be begging. She could practically *hear* his voice now, asking for her help.

She was running out of time. Johanna needed to find a way to hack into the source code before it was too late, but how?

NINE

CINDIRA HAD BEEN WALKING for an hour before she'd realized her ventilator's air had soured. Here, on the edge of civilization, salt water mixed with city grime, creating a pungent cocktail that threatened to turn her stomach. Thinking back on what had happened earlier in the day in Johanna's office further fed her distress. That her stepmother had asked her about the source code was nothing new. For years, Johanna had presented the question in every flavor, from sweet to bitter, but she'd never threatened to endanger Plaxis like that. Surely Johanna must know that Cindira wasn't kidding; most freelance hackers worked for the highest bidder. Sure, they might be able to dig down to the substrate of the servers and release the source code, but Plaxis wouldn't survive long if they did. Why was Johanna suddenly making such unthinkable threats?

Perhaps there was more going on in the vreal than she realized. Cindira hadn't jacked in for nigh on fifteen years. A lot could change in that amount of time. Sure, she overheard things from other people, read stories on both the gossip and journalistic streams about the parties, the sightings, the glitz, the pomp. But news reports couldn't be trusted; she knew that much even as a child. Even Plaxis's own reports were suspect. "Healthy plants do not grow in corrupt soil," her father had told her once when Cindira had caught the company in a public lie. Plaxis policed its own reputation like Authority policed San Francisco's poor: ruthlessly. The building would lay in broken pieces on the ground before anyone would even admit the wall was cracking. No one could see it the way she could, beneath the façade and down to the bone. The only way to do that, however, was to be there.

"Go for Mack." He answered on the tip of the second buzz.

Cindira turned down Market, heading toward the ruins of the San Francisco Ferry Building. "Can you go put in a cameo in the security office and run a little interference?"

"You know most people say hello when they call. It's a basic courtesy."

"So that's a no, then?"

Back at his desk in Plaxis, Mackey barked out a laugh on the other end of the comque. "That's like asking me if I can breathe. Of course, I can. But why do you need me? Your clearance is even higher than mine."

She made the final turn, looking four blocks ahead to where the unkempt majesty of ruined skyscrapers dangled their foundations in the surf. A sunken block more, the clocktower still etched on many of the city's tourist kitsch, illuminated under a gibbous moon, kissed its twin image on the calm waves beneath it. "I don't want Plaxis records tracing any breach back to a source near the Embarcadero."

Apprehension shaded Mack's voice. "You're in that part of town at this time of night?"

"Don't have much choice. If I jack in from one of Plaxis's machines, Johanna will know."

"What you up to, Cin? Going to such lengths to get to a seedy jackpod?"

"Seedy has its advantages."

"Yeah, but the Ferries are where all the bootleggers run their knockoffs that feed the chipheads." Cindira pictured Mackey rubbing his right bicep with his left hand. "Where are you? I'm going to tag out and come down there. I don't like you wandering into that part of town alone."

"Absolutely not, I need you in security. Besides, the chipheads revere me. You think they'd ever do anything to hurt the daughter of their Goddess?"

"If you were actually public about that, maybe not. But don't forget, Cin. Everyone reveres their god until he abandons them." His overly-dramatic sigh told her she'd won him over, even if reluctantly. "What do you need?"

"For no one else to notice the unregistered user walking around Gaia."

"Gaia?" His voice pitched up an octave. "What in the Hell are you going in there for?"

"Because I'm the only one who can."

THE PING-BAILENSON ACT of 2126 consigned all international relations – including war – to Gaia. That had brought peace, but also, questions about where authority and influence truly resided. "The hand that turns the screw, while also making all the screws, and the screwdrivers," one journalist had called it. Gaia might be the one who used the tools which ran the world, but Plaxis owned the garage. Under her father's watch, Cindira trusted that the company upheld its promises to not become involved in politics. Officially, Plaxis only supported the VR system without any compensation. A charitable act. A *humanitarian* act. Cindira still believed that to be true, but what if things had gotten to a quid pro quo state? If that was the case, she wanted to know what that quid was, and for the that, she was going to have to find the quo.

She reached the water as the clocks rolled Tuesday into Wednesday. The Ferry Building had once marked the edge of the city, the place where land gave way to sea. About forty years ago, the sea took a share back, reclaiming sidewalks and cafes. Nearest the shore, you could still find pavers that had been laid down in olden times. Forty yards out, the walls of the first story of the landmark building were being eaten away slowly by saltwater, leaving only the steel girders that kept the upper levels aloft. In time, nature would nibble her way through those, too. Officially, the site was condemned. Unofficially, pirate jackers operated from the famous tower, aware that at any moment, an earthquake, tsunami, or plain bad timing could push out the remaining building beneath them.

Cindira appreciated the reality of it. Foundations toppled all the time; a young girl whose mother died suddenly was all too aware.

"Need passage, love?"

She'd been so fixated on the building, Cindira had neglected to notice the boat bobbing a few feet out, tied to what may have been a lamppost once upon a time. From the darkness, two bloodshot orbs catching ambient light from the city stared out from a face sallow and thin.

"How much to get to the tower?"

"How much you got?"

A spark, then a flicker, and then a flame lit his features.

Cindira's breath caught in her throat at the sight of a mangled twist of sinew and scar tissue, one prominent demarcation that ran from his collarbone, up his neck, and to where the corner of his mouth had healed poorly, leaving the bottom lip longer than the other. On his chin, a tattooed barcode occupied space where once a beard may have grown.

"You're a convict."

"No, love. I'm an ex-con. Survivors have scars." He pulled a long tug from his cigarette and blew out the smoke in a long tunnel. "And heads."

Cindira stilled herself and silenced the tiny voice in the back of her head telling her only an idiot would get into a skiff with an admitted criminal and head into the night on the very waters where her mother died.

"I can give you sixteen for the trip out."

"The trip out is free. It's the trip back that'll cost you."

"Sixteen for that, then."

"Twenty."

"Eighteen."

"Done."

Pulling an oar from the bottom of the boat, he closed the distance over the calm water, offering out a hand at the shore. When Cindira reached for him, intending to slide her fingers over his to steady her step down. She almost fell over when he pulled back.

"Money first."

"You said the ride out was free."

"It is, but what if you never come back?"

She ticked up the agreed-upon fee into the bracelet on her wrist, but then paused before putting her finger on the print reader to slide the funds over. "Doesn't everybody?"

"From the tower? You serious?" When she nodded, he continued. "Some don't. Them's the type that likes to get jacked in, but no intention of ever coming back out."

Chipheads.

Cindira pushed the send signal, and the money transfer was done. This time when he offered his aid, she took it readily. Without sea legs, her arms went wide, holding out to the sides and steadying herself as she sat. "But don't they know their bodies atrophy after a while?"

"They go there to die, love. It's a bit of the point. I mean, all them Buddhists talking about Nirvana, isn't that what they're after? Freeing the mind from the body? Makes me wonder if them dead ones ain't still alive somehow, inside those machines." He looked out across the water, wistful in a way that bordered jealousy.

After a few moments, his focus drew back to her. "Pretty thing like you shouldn't waste your life away in some VR opium den or night club. You parlay the right folk, you could get a sugar, get inside the Kingdom even."

The last thing she wanted was some richie who supplied her with jack time in exchange for money and/or lewd acts.

Her chest rose and fell. "I'm going to jack into Gaia."

"The bloody World Order?" The oarsman guffawed. "Tell you what, I'll give you back half your money and take you back now. No point on you going to the Ferries. None of them can get you in there."

"I don't need them to get me in. I just need use of their jackpods and an agreement to look the other direction."

"The other direction's the only way they know how to look in there." He nodded, puffing on his cigarette even as he continued to row. "You'd need to have some serious connections to jack into a system like that. Or be a crack hacker."

She turned back to the edifice towering above. "I do, and I am."

TEN

"WE DON'T ACCEPT GREENS."

The surly woman who met her at the door—or the gaping hole in the wall that had once been a window—curled a lip as Cindira's finger hovered over her comque. U.S. Dollars, called "greens" for merely anachronistic purposes as the country itself no longer existed, still ruled legitimate markets, but this wasn't exactly Union Square.

"I have crypto." Cindira scrolled through her personal ledgers. "Do you take bot? Or rubis? I can even pass you kartz, if you're looking for something really exotic."

A chill ran up her spine when the wrinkled woman's claw clutched Cindira's hand. "Lots of variety for someone climbing the tower. Who are you, and why would someone like you come about these parts? You think you're setting me up?"

"I'm here for the same reason anyone else comes here." Cindira loaded two hundred kartz into the transfer tray on her comque, then hit send. The Ferrier's own device buzzed on her wrist, indicating receipt. "Because I'm not really here, if you catch me."

The grizzled woman studied the numbers flashing on her wrist. "That's twice the daily rate."

"And all I need is two hours, a private jackpod, the highest bandwidth you got, and the ability to disable any security protocol you have in place."

"No go. Without my walls, all that dirty water comes slushing in."

"Don't worry, I'm going to build new walls. Everything will stay high and dry."

The Madame's face cycled through resolution, doubt, temptation, and, finally, resignation. "Fine, but I'm going to have my hand over the power button, don't care if the sudden evac scrambles your brain or not."

"Fine by me."

"Follow me then."

They walked down a hall with broken tile floors and graffitied walls. Moonlight fell through what must have been an arched glass ceiling at some point. Now, only frame remained, blanketed over by tattered tarps blowing in the wind. Crossing a mezzanine, Cindira's attention hooked onto a familiar set of eyes that pulled her like tractor beams in their direction. The subject of the mural sat in lotus position, her hands open, upturned on her knees. In one hand, a dead earth still smoldered at the edges, and in the other, she held a miniaturized rain forest, verdant and flowing with rivers.

The Madame took turns looking at the mural, then to Cindira. "Anyone ever tell you that you look like her?"

"We're both just Indian is all." Cindira tried to distance any speculation. "Who painted this?"

"Who knows? It's been here longer than I have. The chipheads think her image has the power to keep this building from falling down. The kooks."

Cindira looked back at the stout woman. "You sound like you don't believe it."

"I don't. Just because she invented Gaia doesn't mean she's divine. This building will fall when the universe decides it should, no matter what we do. Just like this planet will die with or without us, no matter how many Omala Grovers it gives birth to."

FOR FIFTEEN YEARS, one question had resurfaced in Cindira's thoughts again and again. If she could ever bring herself to do it, if she could ever go back into that place forever tied to the memory of her mother, would it be like they'd left it that day?

At last, she had her answer.

The room was the same. Modest, with two twin beds and a nightstand. A closet held a collection of clothing and shoes, the fashions just dated enough to be noticeable. The wallpaper: pale yellow and with white primroses. The mirror in the corner faced the door, but even as Cindira sat up, she saw its angle was just enough to reflect not her own bare feet, but those of the woman lying on the other bed.

Her mother's avatar remained right where she'd left it, stretched out on the other bed, as though she may pop into it at any moment. Cindira sat up and waited, half-expecting her mother's eyes to crack open, for her to turn her head her way and say, "Good morning, *pyar beti.* What new thing shall we learn today?"

The Capital City had been her playground then. The Congress, the Hall of Records, the Archives... even the palace where the elected Prince or Princess held court. (She'd heard a rumor that the newest sovereign elected for a five-year term had decided to forgo tradition and simply keep an office in the Congressional Building. The vreal palace had been taken offline at his request.) Oh, she'd never been permitted to *attend* court, but she could *imagine* what that had been like. All of her mother's stories helped, of course.

Outside the city, beyond its fortified walls, combat raged on in the battlefields of the wardomes, but she'd been too young to understand what that meant, too innocent to perceive its discussion in conversation. It was incomprehensible now, that this world her mother created, in which the Capital City and its people shone, was merely a pearl trapped in the mire of the oyster's gullet.

The Grover Gaia residence stood apart from the city, while seemingly embedded into its very heart. A "magic pumpkin," her mother had called it, a parallel reality built with the same source code and paradigms, but not technically embedded in it. Each wardome had been structured much the same. Most of the time, when a person with a vreal world account holder died, any avatar created for them was permanently archived. Omala's would have been too, if not contained in the safety of this bubble.

Before she knew what she was doing, Cindira was on her knees at her mother's bedside, Omala's hand wrapped in her own.

"Mom." Her heart fluttered in her chest. "Um... Hi. I... I know this isn't really you. I get that. But, well... It's been a while and... I've said this at your grave too, but just to say it again: You were... You *are* my hero. I look back on the things you've done and the worlds you created and I... They're just so wonderful. You gave the world such a gift, and the only thing you asked for in return was me. It didn't seem like a fair exchange, but I did my best to make it seem like it was. I'm still trying, but Johanna..."

She bit back the bitterness, refusing to let that poison seep into this moment.

"I want you to know: I'm still watching out. For Plaxis, for Gaia, for the Kingdom. For Dad, when he lets me, but you know how he is."

She imagined her mother laughing, even though the empty avatar remained unchanged.

"Mom, wherever you are, can you watch out for *me*? If you do that, then you're helping to look out for them too. I miss you, and I love you."

She pushed a kiss to Omala's hand, before gently setting it beside her mother's body.

Sunbeams spun of gold and crimson pierced Cindra's eyes as she stepped out of what, looking behind her for a moment, appeared to be a red brick wall. Funny, but she remembered the outside of the 'magic pumpkin' as a wood-framed door with a single pane of stained glass. In fact, she'd seen that door and opened it from the inside just moments before. When she reached for where she thought the doorknob should be, the image blurred. Cindira picked up a piece of stone from a nearby flowerbed and used it to etch a mark. On her return, she'd be certain to know the way out. She could exit the program from anywhere, but if Gaia still had the same security protocols as it'd had when she was younger – as the copied world of the Kingdom still had – the AI embedded into the source code would scan the environment each night at midnight. Any unregistered entity would be wiped clean. If she left her avatar behind, even hidden, she'd never be able to return to it again.

The avenue led to the main square, beyond which another promenade would carry her to Congressional Hall. Few souls roamed the streets this early in the day. The Gaian time zone aligned with the city that had inspired the design of this part of the vreal, The Hague, as it had existed about two hundred or so years before. That also meant, however, that it was hours ahead of the local time in San Francisco. Cindira had always admired this choice made by her mother, not only to design a vreal so intense in its reality as to deceive the human mind, but styled after a period of history in which rich fabric, marbled motifs, and gold-gilded mosaics were all the rage. Every design rang true, from the grand clock tower ticking out the minutes on the palace gate, to the intricately-fitted tiles on the floors within it.

She'd never been taken outside the safety zone of the Capital , so she couldn't know if the wardomes had changed or not. From the nightly shows, where captures of national 'battles' taking place within Gaia doubled as entertainment, she knew that they'd endured, however. Cindira shuddered to think what life was like before her mother's creation, when you lived under the threat of war, anything could hide a bomb, and anyone could be a terrorist. She'd often wondered if living through the fall of London was what had inspired her mother's concept of Gaia in the first place.

Just imagine it: a city that could never be overtaken, and war that could never destroy.

Enough reminiscing, Cindira thought. *To work.*

While his name may have been made up, Cindira suspected there was some truth to Batista's claim about working with the Gaia security forces. As he wasn't Authority, and as it seemed certain Johanna had known as much and let him have access, it was the only thing that made sense. Seeing him in Kaylie's room suggested he'd been working with a supreme level of cybersecurity. It would take one hell of a crack hacker to infiltrate Alsace, and that kind of talent didn't work blue. She supposed it was still possible he was a con artist. If so, was his whole charade full of evil intentions? Still a possibility, but she'd investigate this part of it first.

The Hall of Records occupied a long road of townhouses, three stories high and running on for two blocks near the palace. If she could get inside, Cindira could wire into their records and search through profile photos for one that looked like Batista. It shouldn't be too hard for her to code a model of his face from her memory, then scan the database for close matches. She was a few steps from the stoop leading to the entry when a hand wrapped around her arm and delicately pulled her back.

She wouldn't have to look for Batista's picture. The man stood right before her. Curious, he was dressed the same way he'd been in real life, down to the antiquated watch on his wrist.

He blinked twice, three times. When he spoke, it was both with amusement, and an undertone of rebuke. "Children aren't allowed into this building."

"Children?"

She might be a little on the young side for someone with her abilities and position, but twenty-eight was hardly a child. Only then did Cindira realize that the detective was a lot taller than he'd been when she'd seen him at Plaxis. And his hand must be huge to so easily wrap around her arm with the fingers folding over so much. Maybe her memory wasn't as good as she...

Oh, wait. Wait, no, he was right.

Suddenly the truth struck her. Her avatar had sat unused for fifteen years. Consequently, as was customary, it hadn't been reiterated to represent her real-world aging. From Frank Batista's perspective, she'd still look like her eleven-year-old self. Gaian protocol didn't allow for minor avatars except in the case of actual children. It didn't matter. In fact, it couldn't hurt that she appeared to be her younger self. If Batista recognized her from Plaxis, who knew what trouble that could cause. Tensions between Gaia and her father's company were tense enough. If he thought she were here as a spy...

But she was, wasn't she? Only, not for Plaxis. And it's not like he wasn't at Plaxis snooping around either.

"Are you lost?"

Cindira snapped back to the moment. "Not exactly."

He let go of her arm when he seemed certain she wouldn't bolt. Batista looked around. "You here with a school group or a parent? You know you're not supposed to wander around on your own. Even if it is a virtual environment, security is very tight. Someone might think you were up to something."

"I..." What could she say? "I'm here with my mom, but she's... I lost her."

In the worst of ways.

"Okay, then..." His face broke into a smile, and she felt something melt deep within her. "Let's get you unlost and back to your mother. What's your name?"

"Cin... Cindy," she lied, the quiver of guilt within turning electric when she realized the opportunity it had presented her. "What's yours?"

"Been a while since anyone here had to ask." His head tilted. "Feels a little funny. You sure you don't know?"

He'd said it with such lightness, she wasn't sure if he was being coy or arrogant.

"No, I'm sorry. Should I?"

"So the secrecy protocols are working," he said, seemingly more to himself than her. "That should make Carlos happy. You can call me Francisco."

Francisco, not Frank. She made a mental note to rerun her searches using the amended knowledge. For the moment, she had to be careful not to blow her cover. "That's the same name as the prince, isn't it?"

"It is." Francisco's mouth dropped open in mock surprise. When he wasn't acting like an indifferent authoritarian, he was quite charming. "It's a very common name, though. But I'll let you in on a little secret. He's not as handsome as I am."

No doubt of that. No one knew what the real Prince Francisco looked like. His real-world identity was a state secret, a way of protecting his physical body from harm while he was jacked into Gaia. Cindira was willing to bet, however, that some stuffy old politician couldn't claim such deep brown eyes or have the defined, perfected cheek bones that this Francisco had. Whoever had sculpted his avatar should be given a major award.

Reminding herself that she'd seen Francisco in the real, however, she realized that the artist responsible for this work was one of divine origins.

Or, at least, *really* good genetics.

"Now, where should you be?" He surveyed the street. "Don't suppose you know which direction you came from?"

"I was with my class. We're touring the Capital."

One of Francisco's eyebrows took on a precarious angle, telling her she'd messed up somehow. In her defense, Cindira would openly admit lying wasn't an art in which she was well-practiced.

"I thought you said your mom brought you here?"

Damn it, she had said that, hadn't she? "Oh, she did. She's one of the chaperones. The last place I remember being with everyone was in Ferreira Square."

With balled fists on hips, Francisco stared at a patch of ground. "Ferreira Square? You sure about that?"

"Pretty sure. It's where they swore in the first congress, right? I recognized it from my... lesson docs?"

"Is that so?"

An invisible hand reached into her stomach and squeezed. What had she said wrong now? "I think, or maybe I—*ahh!*"

The experience of pain inside of Gaia? That was new. It was not, however, welcome. As Francisco gripped Cindira by the wrist, squeezing away her confidence, storm clouds gathered in his eyes.

"What's the name of your school?"

"My..." *Whimper.* "Musk Preparatory!"

Not her actual high school, but the one her mother had wanted her to go to before she died. Johanna had had other plans, ones that took her far away from San Francisco and her father. Still, she shouldn't have said it.

"There is no group here today from Musk Preparatory!" His teeth clenched, and with it, his grip. "And you couldn't have been in Ferreira Square. Your people destroyed it two weeks ago!"

"Destroyed it?" She fell to her knees, gasping. "*My* people?"

With a twist, her hands flattened to the street. Francisco pulled his comque to his mouth. "Security, triangulate my location and identify the user nearest me. Seems one of the hackers has crawled out of the shadows."

"I'm not a hacker." Or at least, she wasn't a hacker with the intention to harm, and that made her something different than what he implied.

Didn't it?

"Then tell me who you really are and what your people are trying to accomplish by destroying Gaia piece by piece."

Cindira was too stunned to respond. *Someone's destroying my mother's work? But how? The Capital City is safe, the code is unbreakable—*

"Warning: explosion imminent. Vacate area."

The matter-of-fact tone of the emergency system notification brought them both to a standstill. Francisco, because of the implication, she reckoned. Cindira, because the voice was her mother's.

Francisco pulled Cindira's arm, jerking her away. "Hurry, run! Get out of—"

Wait. He was *helping* her now? Just after accusing her of being an anarchist, he was trying to save her?

She'd have listened to him, if it had been within her power. But she couldn't run. She couldn't move. Cindira couldn't do... anything.

Intense, utter pain wracked her body from the inside out. Before her, Francisco called out for the briefest of moments. And then he was gone.

Only when Cindira hit her head against the glass of the jackpod and felt the real-world sweat dripping from her forehead did she realize she was out. Not by choice, but by force. And she could never go back to Gaia again.

There'd be nothing to go back to. Her avatar would have been destroyed in the explosion.

ELEVEN

SCOTIA MACAVOY GRABBED the bat at her bedside. The Inner Mission wasn't a den of criminal activity, but common sense dictated certain precautions. Her pulse slowed as she realized the person pounding on her door at 3 AM wasn't trying to get in by force, but by desperation. Nonetheless, she remained vigilant as she tiptoed to the door and flicked on the preview screen. A hologram a mere few inches tall displayed at eye level, represented the woman on the other side.

"Cindira?" Scotia flung the door open, catching her breathless friend as she collapsed into her arms. "Oh, my god, what happened?"

Cindira struggled to get the words out. "I ran... here... once I got to... shore."

"Shore? What do you mean shore? Were you out on the bay?"

Cindira recovered her feet and drove forward. But not for the couch, as Scotia had supposed, but for the TV. The wall flickered to life as Cindira scrolled through the stations, past late-night advertisements and reruns of the ancient programs people called flat flickers.

"No, the Ferries." Wide-eyed, Cindira turned on her. "Local channels?"

Scotia closed the door and called on her in-home artificial intelligence assistant. "Tyra, tune to channel six, please."

Tyra quickly obeyed her master, even though her master had no idea why the hell she was asking.

Cindira's breathing normalized as she and Scotia took a seat on the couch. On the wall, the local channel appeared to be showing a rerun of a daytime soap, only with the mostly Caucasian and Latino actors modulated to Chinese.

"Impossible."

"Oh, wait, that's my fault. I was practicing my Mandarin earlier. Tyra, please switch the spoken language to American."

"I don't mean the language." Cindira was on her feet again, pacing. "Tyra, bring up a preview screen of all news channels, local, national, and international."

Two beeps proceeded Tyra's serene twill. "Guest access authorized?"

Scotia acknowledged it. The wall segmented into dozens of tiny boxes, each displaying a thumbnail version of the channel it represented. Cindira pecked at the wall, wiping away options with her gestures, growing more restless when each image increasing in size proved to be as unsatisfactory as the last.

"No, no! It's not possible! Someone has to know. *Someone has to be covering it!*"

Scotia studied her friend's reaction, reading the confusion through a furrowed brow that soon turned into a huff of frustration.

"Tyra, TV off. Cindira—" Scotia pivoted. "—it's three-thirty in the morning. What's this about?"

Her friend ran a hand through her silken black hair. "There was an explosion. Inside Gaia. Thirty... No! *Forty* minutes ago."

"There are always explosions in Gaia. That's kinda the point of the wardomes."

Cindira shook her head. "Not them. In the Capital City. I was just there, I was—"

"Wait, you were *in* Gaia?" Confusion wasn't quite the right term for what Scotia was feeling. Bewilderment? That might do.

"Yes! I saw it. I was there. I..." She swallowed, all color draining from her olive complexion. "I was where it happened. I... blew up."

"Don't be ridiculous. It couldn't have..." But the look in her friend's face told her she wasn't lying. Or at least, as far as Cindira was concerned, she was speaking God's honest truth. But that didn't make any sense. "You'd need an exceptionally high security clearance to be able to get into Gaia without some sort of official invite or sponsorship."

"I hacked in."

"Oh, well then." What other holes could Scotia poke in this to get her friend to come back to reality? "But even then, you'd need an avatar, and you told me that you don't have one."

"I said I don't *currently* have one. I did have one before my mother died."

"So, let me get this straight..." Scotia pushed the thumb and index finger of her left hand into her temple. "You've had an avatar inside of Gaia, hidden somewhere and no one found it? Where?"

"Inside a magic pumpkin." When Scotia stared at her, slack-jawed, Cindira continued. "That's what we call the ancillary code nodes that vine off the main platform. Well, not *magic* anymore, just pumpkins. They run parallel to the vreal but aren't technically part of it."

"Right." Scotia pushed an index finger into her chin. "And to stay off grid, last night you went to the Ferries to hang out with a bunch of VR addicts and hack your way into Gaia."

"Not technically into Gaia. I'm not sure if even *I'm* capable of that. I went into a pumpkin where my mom used to keep our avatars when we weren't in the vreal. It, in turn, bridged to Gaia. I was hoping to access some records embedded there so I could figure out who Frank Batista really was, but then... I don't know, he was just suddenly *there*, standing in front of me. At first, he was being nice, and then he figured out that I wasn't who I said I was."

"And who did you say you were?"

Cindira's eyes rolled to the ceiling as she searched her memory. "I just said my name was Cindy. But he figured out I wasn't a little kid like I said I was. That avatar? It's one from fifteen years ago, when I was eleven. Anyway, he started claiming that I was the one responsible for blowing up Ferreira Square, and before I could figure out what he was talking about—" Cindira cupped her hands before her before fanning out her fingers and drifting them apart. "*Boom.*"

"So the very guy you were looking for just... happened to find you? And then everything exploded?" One eye squinted. "Are you sure this wasn't just a nightmare you were having? It is the middle of the night."

"I considered that, but the money for the jackpod rental at the Ferries is gone from my account. Look, Scotia, I know it sounds crazy but..."

Cindira's voice trailed off as her eyes went unfocused. Scotia knew that look, the one that said her friend wasn't thinking in words, but in code. After a few moments, she snapped her fingers in time with the lightning striking her brain. "That must be it! It *didn't* happen. What I perceived as an explosion was just a security measure. The system recognized my avatar as an unregistered entity and blasted me out. Yes. Yes, that must be it. It couldn't have been a *real* explosion, right? How would that even happen there?"

Scotia pulled at the threads she could grasp. "Gaia is a platform designed, in part, for mankind to fight its wars in an environment where no one would be actually hurt. You want to know how an explosion happened *there*?" She pushed a hand against her friend's brow. "What did you take? Did someone sneak you something?"

"I'm fine." Cindira's frigid fingers pulled Scotia's hand from her brow. "I must sound like one of the chipheads in your studies."

"*VR addict*, not chiphead. And no, not really. You're not paranoid enough." Scotia shrugged. "I don't think anyone gets addicted in just one night. Just tell me what happened, as best as you remember it."

Cindira nodded before scooting back to take a seat on the sofa. "Okay, so I was at Plaxis, fixing up Kaylie's dress inside the Kingdom, through the Sink—"

"What?" Scotia held up a hand as she pushed her way into the conversation. "I thought we agreed you were going to tell her to go to hell if she did that again. Cindira, you've got to learn to stand up for yourself. Stop letting the Terrible Two push you around."

"That's not the point. Just listen, please?" Her begging proved pitiful enough to win sympathy. And silence. "I was in the simulator, when Frank Batista just showed up, looking all around Kaylie's room."

Scotia's hands went to her gaping mouth. "Did he see you?"

"No, he was like a... like a... ghost, or something."

"There's no such thing as ghosts. Not in the vreal world, not in this one. Besides, you put up the security parameters around Alsace yourself. There's no way someone could have gotten in without you having validated their profile."

"You mean, the way no one could get inside Gaia without the right credentials?" The brunette laughed under her breath at her own rebuke. "There aren't many as good at hacking Plaxis systems as I am, but there has to be a few people out there. But if Frank... *Francisco*, it actually turns out, were such a crack hacker, why would he risk exposing his identity by coming to Plaxis, anyway?"

A diode in Scotia's memory illuminated. She grabbed her comque from its charger on the side table. "I may be terrible with faces, but I'm great with names. I don't know a *Frank* Batista but—" Scotia grinned when she found what she was looking for. "I'd be tempted to tell you this guy was feeding you bull, but adapting to an English standard rather than a Spanish one is more redaction than dishonesty."

"You're saying he was lying..." Cindira's head cocked to the side. "... by telling a *version* of the truth?"

Her red hair bounced on her shoulders as she nodded. "It's something *politicians* are famous for. Here, take a look."

Only a few weeks before, Scotia had been asked to present a report inside of Gaia on her research, at a session attended by several high-ranking politicians. In general, and for security, the representations of avatars of such elite were kept secret from outsiders. Still, Scotia managed to get permission to click off one picture, with the caveat that it was for private use only.

"He wasn't introduced, but he came into the hearing room halfway through my presentation, and you could just tell he was important by the way everyone got all awkward in their seats. Afterward one of the congressmen told me who he was. I don't think anyone realized I got him in my picture, or they probably wouldn't have let me keep it." She double tapped her comque, making the tiny image on the flexible screen on her wrist pop out as a proportional holographic display. "That's him, isn't it?'

Her friend's bloodshot eyes nearly popped out of their sockets. Cindira lunged forward, grabbing Scotia's wrist and angling the tiny projected image to a better vantage point. "It is! Who is he?"

Most people who worked with Cindira Tieg considered her a genius. But as with most geniuses, a surplus of savvy had been paid through a debit against other areas of knowledge. In her case: current events. Scotia didn't consider it a fault. It was what it was. Cindira could ramble off from memory Pi to sixty places or recite on demand the latest policies adopted by the International Commission on Alt-Reality Standards, but ask who the current mayor of San Francisco was or which two actors were rumored to be dating, and she threw you anime eyes.

All that was left was for Scotia to state the obvious. "Cindira, you were talking to Francisco Batista de la Reina, the Prince of Gaia."

Denial took control of Cindira's body, making her hands shake. "Impossible. Why would the prince make his avatar look exactly like he really looks?"

"Why indeed? Not that *I'm* complaining." Scotia bit her lip as she again double tapped the device on her wrist. The image disappeared, as did Scotia's patience with middle-of-the-night intrigues. "Questions, I'm afraid, that will wait for a more respectable time of the morning. We both need to get some rest. Stay here, at least until sunrise. We'll start figuring it out together. If you need something to help you sleep..."

"I don't."

Scotia set her comque back on the charger. "Good. You know, it's too bad I didn't know about that avatar you had. I might have wanted to borrow it. Hardly anyone gets to go into the high security zone. Why haven't you visited Gaia all these years?"

"Because I don't belong there, Scotia. I'm just a code writer. I'm not a diplomat, and I'm certainly not a warrior."

Scotia smiled. "Yeah, tell that to Barrel."

TWELVE

TRY AS SHE MAY, SLEEP refused to come. Cindira lay on Scotia's pull-out sofa, her hands laced over her stomach, her eyes making patterns of the random blots splotched all over the textured ceiling. Questions were demanding hobgoblins, ones which seem to double with every answer she suggested.

Why had Batista shown up at Plaxis alone, claiming to be nothing more than a detective? Why not just send an actual Gaia security agent? Was the prince in the habit of traipsing about the real without guards? Maybe he couldn't trust his own security detail? But if he wasn't communicating with them, who had helped him get into such a secure part of the Kingdom? Why was he so interested in the source code?

Why had getting booted from Gaia felt like an explosion?

Cindira wished she could shut down her mind the way she could shut down one of her computers. As she heard the sound on the floor beside her, however, she was glad to be awake. If not, the shock of something scurrying across the room and leaping up on the end of the mattress might have set her off screaming. Instead, she moved with the stealth of a ninja, slowly extending her arm to the side table where the cup of water Scotia had given her before going back to bed sat empty. Fingers curled around the plastic vessel. Rat or mouse or squirrel even, she'd probably miss hitting it, but hopefully she could scare it away.

The creature began to scuttle, zipping left, then right, inching up the bed. Cindira gave herself a moment of pep talk, drew down a lungful of courage, and sprang up as she simultaneously heaved the tumbler.

Lamps flickered on overhead as the sensors along the walls tripped. The light brought no meaning, and only further illuminated her confusion.

The mouse stared at the intended weapon where it had landed

on the mattress next to him. Turning to Cindira, his tiny black eyes blinked twice before he opened his mouth and did the impossible.

"Well, *that* was uncalled for!"

Cindira scrambled back against the couch cushions. "I'm going crazy." Hallucinations were common among chipheads. She didn't jack in *that* much, did she? She pushed fingers into her forehead. "Maybe I have a tumor? *Oh my god, I have a tumor.*"

"Miss, you do not have a tumor. In fact, I was able to complete a full diagnostic of all your vital systems when you logged into your avatar last night and can confirm that, other than typical aging, your health has experienced no significant changes in the last fifteen years. By the way, it was about time you showed up. I was beginning to think you were never jacking in again."

"You ran a diagnostic? When I was in..." *Gaia.* Which she hacked into illegally. Well, technically, entered without direct authorization, which was basically the same thing. "I don't know what you're talking about. More than that, I don't know *how* you're talking. Mice. Don't. Talk."

"That's true." The mouse blinked twice, wiggled its little nose, and took a few steps forward. "But then again, I'm not really a mouse, as you'll recall. It's me, Laporte."

"My issue isn't remembering your name. The issue is that you are *talking* and I am *crazy.*"

The mouse fell into deep completion. Which, of course, a rodent could probably manage if he could also talk. "You must have blocked me out, associated me with your mother around the time of her death. I'm not sure how to proceed now. The possibility that you would have no recollection of me is not one for which I made any contingencies. Human memory has such horrendous design flaws. In light of that, the best option, in my opinion, would be to enact the parameter of the least likely scenario, for which I did prepare."

Despite the idiocy of engaging in conversation with a figment of her imagination, curiosity got the better of Cindira. "What was the least likely scenario you thought of?"

"That you would attempt to smash me with a large, heavy object. With your permission, may I run that scenario?"

Why did she nod?

"Very good." The mouse turned a full circle, almost as if resetting itself. "Miss, I beg you, put down the *name of heavy object* and listen. I've come to warn you, you are in great danger."

THIRTEEN

MUSCLES TIGHT, PULSE racing, nails digging into the heel of his hand, drawing blood.

Medics descended as soon as his consciousness shifted realities, but that moment—the one the blaze blew away his skin and shredded his body—held eternity on the balance of a crescent.

Francisco seethed as the real-world reclaimed him and his conscious mind uncoupled from Gaia. He shut his eyes against the confusion, willing it away, telling himself to feel truth and not the dream. He had *not* been in an explosion. He had *not* been blown into a dozen pieces. He had *not* just watched an intruder masquerading as a child be killed. *Dios,* he prayed it hadn't been an actual child. It was mere vreal world illusion. His avatar had been sacrificed at the altar of peace, not his mortal form. Avatars were replicable, rewritable.

But wired into the system, his mind still processed the pain as though it had happened, and it hurt like a son of a bitch.

Flailing arms and a wracked body surrendered as his guards pinned him down, keeping him from hurting himself and any others trying to attend him. Carlos's voice gave him a beacon on which to grasp.

"You're back, Your Highness. It wasn't real. This is real. This is the world."

He clung to the truth as his lifesaver, conquering his panicked mind. "Explosion," he gasped out. "Another explosion." His hand went to his father's old watch on his wrist, as if the destruction of it in avatar form had somehow destroyed the real one as well.

"Yes, sir," Carlos confirmed. "We're looking into the details now, but we know. We're already rebuilding your avatar. It should be ready by the end of the day, if you wish to return."

Another pull on his limited budget. Royal avatars, compiled from scratch and embedded with hundreds of security modifications, required highly-skilled coders. His predecessors had only needed such services once, when assuming office. This was the third time in his term that he'd call upon them – and he hadn't even served six months into his five-year term. He'd just have to pull funds from another of Gaia's programs.

Again.

As the tension began to ease and Francisco regained his senses, his thoughts turned to the consequences. He pushed the security guards and doctor gently away.

"Damage report."

"A few buildings in the immediate vicinity, and the street, of course. The architects estimate Congressional Hall will fully restore itself in twelve days."

He doubted it. Whatever strips of code the rebels had used to blow up Ferreira Square left the area unrepairable. The explosion had destroyed it down to the source code, a play that Plaxis itself admitted it couldn't touch. Francisco expected the Congressional office buildings would prove to have sustained the same kind of damage.

Someone was trying to destroy Gaia piece by piece. Only this time, the fact that they'd sent in an agent to intercept him in the target area suggested their goals might not end with the platform; they might extend to the Congress itself.

Carlos slid shoes on to Francisco's feet. "We've called off sessions for the day and alerted both Congress and their staff, as a precaution. I've asked each of their offices to report any—"

"Damn it, Carlos, tell me about the girl!" He sat up, shaking the sweat from his hair. "Do we know who she was yet?"

Carlos's dark brow fretted. "The girl, sir?"

"The one whose arm I was holding when the explosion hit. We need to find out how she wandered so far into the secure zone alone. Get out across the wires, too, and make sure no one hears about this latest attack."

Maybe that had been her purpose: to be a witness. After Gaia officials had been able to squash the news of the previous three attacks in the city from leaking, the rebels must be growing frustrated, not getting the righteous outrage they had expected. If there was a witness, however, one who likely had been backing up her POV on some external source so she could run to the media with it later, that cat would soon be out of the bag. Unless they found her first.

When Carlos stayed mum, Francisco's anger finally broke. "Come on, people, it's a basic username query. I know you don't know code, but you can handle a whois request, can't you?"

"Sir, it's not that. It's just..." The valet swallowed his nerves. "As I already said, you were the only user in the vicinity at the time. There wasn't a child. There wasn't anyone else."

"But that's impossible. She was..."

A dark truth hit the prince's mind all at once. "She was the bomb, Carlos."

"Sir?"

Francisco slid off the bed and hurried to one of the system panels in the control room of the Gaia jackpod. A few taps in the historical ledger brought up the stories he remembered reading a few weeks ago in the dossier prepared for him. Since Gaia's launch, so few real-world skirmishes occurred, the practice of many of the ways of resistance and war had been forgotten in the previous generation. At last, he found the file and pulled it up.

"A suicide bomber," Francisco declared, enlarging the article so his deputy could see. "Innocence, Carlos. It's probably the one trap that works on me."

"But sir," the deputy continued, "even if she was a suicide bomber, *she* would still show up in the records. There were no other avatars in the region of the explosion."

Francisco gnashed his teeth. He knew what he knew, no matter what the system reported. "I'm almost starting to think your advice to activate my bodycam inside the platform wasn't so crazy."

Hope lit Carlo's eyes. "I'll do so immediately, Your Majesty."

"No!" Francisco held up a hand. "I said *almost*. I won't be watched like some sort of caged animal." Though his attaché's intentions were pure, the prince knew that once the feed existed, it could be exploited. Keeping him safe may end up putting him in more danger. The body politic required a certain portion of its time to be spent in the shadows to stay healthy. "But I don't understand why the system didn't detect that user."

Had it been a glitch? Had the child not really been there? She couldn't have been a VAPOR, could she? As far as he knew, the human iteration of Virtual Automated Persons, Objects, and Relics couldn't lie. Not only that, but VAPOR "people" were marked between the eyes, a mirrored bhindi revealing them as what they really were. The child had no such marker.

Francisco grabbed a bottled water from the fridge under his desk and took a swig. "Was she a ghost in the machine?"

"Sir?"

The prince turned. "Omala Grover wrote about it in some of her early theoretical work, the ones in her university files that were never published. She theorized that if a person were to die in the real while they were logged in to a robust platform, the neural emulator would effectively allow their avatar to carry on without any knowledge that the body and soul it was based on had passed. There would no longer be a connection from outside the program; our current interfaces wouldn't see the user as being in the space because, technically, they wouldn't be, just their avatar would."

Every additional word made Carlos's features twist a little more. "But what you're saying then, is that this girl who approached you..."

"Might have been already dead," the prince completed the conclusion for him. "But that doesn't mean someone couldn't have found a way to lift her POV data and store it somewhere. Damn it, come to think of it, she might have been an innocent all along. She sure did seem surprised when I turned on her."

And when the building exploded, he *had* seen the panic in her eyes.

"It's just a theory. See what our analysts have to say about it."

Francisco dropped the empty bottle into the recycling bin and wiped his mouth with his sleeve. The taste of frustration remained. How often did he seem to know more about the vreal than the so-called experts he'd inherited with his office? Then again, none of them had had his advantage: none of them had been tutored in their youth by Omala Grover herself.

"We'll figure that part out later," he said after a moment. "For now, just make sure the story doesn't get out. If I find out Johanna Tiegs knows how far the rebels have been able to damage us before I tell her myself, I'm going to be pissed."

FOURTEEN

"ASLA, YOU HERE?"

The house kept its silence. Cindira hadn't expected the old nanny to be home at this time of day; she'd be in the main house, working until five or six. Despite the fact that Cindira begged her to stop, that she didn't need to, that she'd beg Johanna to hire a different housekeeper. But if there was one thing Asla refused to do, it was to put Cindira into a position where she'd need to ask "the old harpy" for anything.

"The coast is clear. Come on."

Cindira reached into her coat pocket and opened her hand. Laporte's tiny feet tickled her palm. The tug of its little claws surprised her. For something that wasn't even real, how could it still be so authentic? She took a seat at the kitchen bar as she set it on the countertop. Just like a real mouse, it set about his grooming with hasty urgency in between polite conversation.

"Thank you, madame, though we must find another way for me to travel with you. Not that your coat pocket is unpleasant, only I do not like being unable to see."

"Sorry, but I wasn't prepared to be an animal carrier." She grabbed an apple from a bowl of fruit and took a bite, continuing to talk around a full mouth. "Tell me again why you don't want Asla to see you. She must remember you, even if I didn't."

"We don't know who we can or can't trust yet." As much as a botic mouse could, Laporte looked apologetic. "For now, my continued existence must remain need-to-know."

"Just out of curiosity, does that include anyone else besides me?"

"Perhaps, but I won't risk exposure to find out. In any case, I haven't spoken to anyone in many years. If those who knew of me are still in the city, they have no reason to believe I endure." It blinked twice. "And I've only come to you now because your recent actions made it necessary. I am doing you no favors to be near you. If my presence is discovered, I fear the repercussions."

The context of that comment did not elude her. No doubt Johanna would love to get her hands on something with so much direct knowledge of Omala's work. "Just how long have you been monitoring me?"

"From a distance, since your mother died. But when you started working at Plaxis, I came back to the city. Luckily, nothing you did put you in harm's way. Until last night."

So much had happened all at once, Cindira at first didn't remember the major life moment less than twelve hours ago. "I don't understand why visiting Gaia would be such a big deal. I've been there before."

"Not since the Kingdom launched. The fact that an explosion occurred precisely where you were during the brief time you were there? I don't believe it's coincidence."

"Are you saying I was the target?" She nearly choked as she gulped down an oversized chunk of fruit. "One, why would someone be trying to blow up my avatar? And two, I didn't know I was going until about 10 PM last night. I don't see how they'd know to expect me."

As much as a mouse could grimace, Laporte did. "That is a query for which I haven't found a reasonable explanation."

"Someone had a bot looking for my neural network signature." Her analytical brain shot into gear. "The question is…who, and for how long?"

"That's two questions, actually." The mouse managed to shake its head. "It is also possible that the attack was indeed meant for the prince, and your presence mere coincidence. After all, the other explosions clearly had nothing to do with you."

"*Other* explosions?" Cindira shot to her feet. When she'd learned there'd been one before her arrival, that was frightening enough. "So Gaia has covered up other attacks? How?" Cindira ran her hands through her thick, black hair. "And how do *you* know any of this?"

"Because I'm Laporte."

Its answer was so simple, it took her a moment to realize she had actually heard correctly. "*Right.*"

"Madame, I was your mother's botic. The purpose behind my design should make the answer obvious."

"But you're not like any other botic I've seen. They're simple devices for people who want a pet without having to feed or clean up after it. Okay, yeah, I've seen a few high-end ones, like the ones hospitals use to cover staff shortages or drop into natural disaster zones. But you'd need to be a hundred times bigger to be one of them. Besides, I'm still not entirely sure I haven't gone insane and am imagining you right now. This could all be a dream, my mind creating ways to rationalize the trauma of having been blasted into pieces last night."

Cindira remembered the mouse she'd seen in the arena as she'd fought Barrel. And again, the one that crossed her path outside her own gate. Oh, and there had been that one that someone seen in the elevator when Batista had visited Plaxis. San Francisco was a city; rodents weren't uncommon, but that seemed like a lot of close encounters in such a short time. Was her brain taking the coincidence and creating this fantasy as a form of self-protection? Or was there something else going on?

"Do you believe that's what's happening?" Laporte waited patiently for her answer.

"I have a near-perfect memory. I'm famous for it, actually. That being said, I've remembered things that never happened before, but I've rarely forgotten something that had."

Laporte continued. "Even if you did remember, it may not help. You thought I was a toy, no matter how many times your mother would firmly remind you I was anything but."

"In my defense, I considered most objects toys. The whole world was my playground, and what I couldn't find, I made up. I used to tell everyone that I had too many dreams to waste time awake."

The past kindled in her memory, a mostly happy childhood in which she'd been precocious and curious and brave and inquisitive, and her mother had encouraged her every impulse to learn, to dream, to explore.

As long as she was in bed on time each night.

"Why did she make you look like that, by the way?" Cindira asked, pushing back memories as she tossed the apple core into the garbage. "I mean, you are an impressive piece of tech. I don't think I've seen a botic anywhere near as realistic as you. Definitely not as small. Why make you look like a dirty street rodent?"

"Affronts to my personal sense of self-worth aside, it was a protective measure." The mouse hedged its answer. "But your question is your answer: I'm designed to resemble something so ubiquitous, I'd be overlooked. No one would look at me and think I was a device capable of monitoring Gaia anytime, day or night. That I could be omnipresent inside of the world, your mother's portal into her creation. I can tap all its records, search logs, review—"

Cindira jumped up. "You can access the source code!" She covered her own mouth when she realized what she'd said, as though someone might be listening.

"Access, but not edit. I am a read-only device."

Still, the power of the source code wasn't necessarily its parts, it was its power when those parts were put to use. "If Johanna knew, she'd be after you in the blink of her surgically-sculptured eyes."

"Not Mrs. Tieg alone. There are others who would also relish an opportunity to hack your mother's work. No one's VR programs have ever been so well designed. Just look at what Plaxis was able to do making a copy of Gaia, and that was only using it as a base and building atop of it. It made your mother furious to find out what Rex and Johanna had done behind her back."

Weakened with the weight of a truth she had suspected all her life, Cindira sank into a nearby chair. "So my father lied; the Kingdom *wasn't* my mother's idea."

"No, and if she hadn't died that night, I'm certain she would have found a way to destroy it."

The echo of memories reverberated in Cindira's head. She didn't remember Laporte, or did she? She had always had a vague memory of someone accompanying her mother to the party on Angel Island the night she died, but those who were there reported Omala had been alone.

"Were you with her when it happened?"

"I was wondering when that would come up." The mouse's head dipped. "It is with deepest regrets that I must tell you I do not know what happened. At the time your mother fell into the water, I was running some rather complex tasks that temporarily shut down my animatronic functions. When I woke up, so to speak, I was floating in the Bay and low on battery. I was able to make it to shore after a few days of swirling around in the tides, but by then your mother was no more. I am sorry, by the way. For your loss, I mean. I know it's been many years, but I do not doubt the pain remains."

The pain of losing the most important person in the world to you? Of being ripped from your childhood home and sent to boarding school thousands of miles away within months? Of your father abandoning his place in your life to raise another woman's children with tenderness and affection while barely giving you the time of day? Of being forced to devote your working life to supporting a program you'd just learned exploited your mother's work without her consent?

Yes, the pain lingered.

"Thank you, Laporte." She inhaled through her nose, centering her thoughts. "You said I was in great danger. What did you mean?"

"You have the same liability that I have. You can access the source code that underlies Gaia and the Kingdom."

She choked on the accusation. "You know that's not true."

It is true, a voice deep within her said.

An even deeper voice shot back, *I know the* language *of the source code, that doesn't mean I can access it!*

Laporte's little white head tipped to the side. "Perhaps you've forgotten that as well. Perhaps, like your memories of me, it's there somewhere, buried, like having the map to a secret treasure, but no ship or shovels to unearth it."

She wasn't sure what kind of reaction he was waiting for, so she said nothing. After a few moments, however, the mouse roused himself from his reverie and changed the subject.

"Did you not receive the package?"

Her nose wrinkled. "What package?"

"The one with the silicone slippers. It was sent here several days ago."

The silicone slippers? "Those weird slip-on shoes?"

Cindira jumped up and rounded the corner of the kitchen. The box still lay on the counter where a few days previously, Kaylie had eyeballed and ridiculed the contents with the most dismissive tone she could muster. Cindira snatched the items from the box and sped back to the mouse.

"They're here, though I'm not really sure what I'm supposed to do with a pair of glass shoes."

"They're not intended to be worn in the real as footwear. You're to wear them more like stockings inside your regular shoes. And they're more than they appear. They're wearable jackpods, though obviously not *pods*, per se."

"Wearable jackpods?" Cindira blew a raspberry. "There's no such thing."

"There are no others, that is for certain," Laporte said. "One researcher in India came close to developing something, but he made a fatal flaw in the design. He thought the shoes should be jackpod and processor, in addition to VR renderers."

That was it, the fantasy died. "I hate to tell you this, but those are the three essential elements of achieving a VR presence, so he was kinda right."

"Oh, that *is* completely correct. But they need not be all in the device itself. In fact, outsourcing the processor is what makes the technology possible."

"But even with that being true – and I don't see how that would work unless the processor was in constant, close proximity – it doesn't solve the problem of energy. The amount of power needed would—"

"Be derived from a combination of solar and kinetic energy harvesting," Laporte again interrupted. "I know you think we're having a theoretical conversation right now, madame, but you don't seem to understand that the device you're holding was how your mother accessed the worlds she created. You're right about one thing, though. The processor could not be small enough to fit into a shoe."

"Where is it then?"

The mouse blinked twice. "I'm looking at her."

FIFTEEN

FOR THE SECOND TIME in as many weeks, Francisco Batista de le Reina, Elected Prince of Gaia, walked into the corner office of the woman who held him and world peace hostage in every way but physically.

"Hello, Johanna."

The blonde snake removed her glasses and looked up from her desk, grinning. "Your Highness?" Something about the way she said it made it sound like an insult. "How delightful to see you again. And so soon! To what do I owe this unexpected pleasure?"

He didn't wait for an invitation to assume the guest chair across from her desk. "You know why I'm here." He unbuttoned his suit coat and crossed his legs, leaning back in the chair to lengthen his body.

"I can only assume you intend to pass yourself off as an investigator and snoop around again. A little friendly advice, though: eventually, you're going to cross paths here with someone else besides me who knows who you really are, and then your cover is going to be blown."

Her mild attempt at a threat failed to land. Francisco pressed on. "There's been another bombing outside of the wardomes in Gaia. This time, two avatars were destroyed, and mine was one. So, I ask you the same question that I did before."

She folded her arms over her chest and gave him her undivided attention. "And my answer is the same. Or did you think I was lying?"

"You, lie?" Francisco chuckled and swiped the air. "I'm sure you don't think that's what I'm suggesting."

"So, you finally believe that I don't have access to the source code? Good. Not a single person in this building does."

"That right there, Johanna." Francisco snapped and pulled himself to the edge of his chair. "*That* is the kind of hedged comment that lets you skate around the truth, isn't it? *No one in this building.* Do you know what that makes me think about? About how long it's been since anyone's seen your husband, in this building or anywhere else."

He'd plucked a string with that move, making Johanna buzz. The blonde placed two hands on the desk and methodically pushed herself back, standing slowly.

"Just to clarify, Your Highness, are you suggesting that my husband is a cyberterrorist using knowledge he's denied having to destroy Plaxis's gift to humanity, that he's enabling such evil, or merely that I'm lying about his having such knowledge?"

"How could he *not* know about the source code?" Francisco demanded. "Wasn't Plaxis and Gaia the result of his work with Omala Grover? Given the fact that they were married at the time, I find it hard to believe he's completely in the dark."

The momentary ghost of past grudges and insecurity erupted onto Johanna's face. As quickly as it came, it fled. The wrinkles around her eyes grew deeper as she pulled on a smile and sharpened her good graces. She rounded her desk with deliberate steps.

"I don't often share my personal feelings with anyone other than my husband, and on occasion, my own children. I hope you understand that, as I'm about to tell you something I've never shared with anyone else."

The prince acknowledged her with a dip of his chin. "Enlighten me."

"I detest Gaia."

The comment took him aback, both mentally and physically. "Why?"

"I could say because maintaining its infrastructure and hardware is a nightmare, both logistically and financially. How its bandwidth eats up precious resources I'd rather dedicate to our for-profit endeavors. Or I could tell you that playing host to the world's most advanced wardomes makes us the constant target of hackers and shadow players. All these things are true, of course, but I'm afraid the real answer is very petty. I hate Gaia because it was *hers*. Because forever more, all the work I do will benefit the creation of the woman who, even fifteen years after her death, my husband still loves, no matter how much he denies it. I would rather it died, and with it, the constant reminder Rex deals with of just how wonderful his ex-wife was."

She meant it. God help him, but she meant every word.

"And despite all this," Johanna continued, "I keep it going. I diminish our profit margins, skive from our investors, and raise billions of greens a year in charity drives, to keep it going, because when it dies, I'm afraid my husband's heart—and our marriage—will die with it."

She settled back into her chair, leaning her forehead into hands pressed as if in prayer. When her closed eyes flew open again, Johanna reengaged her mask of slighted malevolence.

"Rex doesn't know how to access the source code, and neither do I. We know no more Purusha Plus than any other coder in this building. No one knew in completeness Purusha Prime and how to access the source code except for Omala. As much as I detested her, I'm not bitter enough to say she was a fool or to deny her genius. No doubt she would have made plans to transfer her knowledge had she not slipped off that dock and gotten herself nearly decapitated by a boat, but she never got that chance. If there's someone, somewhere, who can get to the code, I haven't been able to find them. And so, I live each day in castles built of sand, knowing that someday, everything we've heaved on top of Omala's work will collapse. For now, I'm just as determined to weed out whoever is attacking inside of it as you are."

And there it was. She'd tipped her hat. And now, Francisco had to decide if he'd do the same. Despite having no doubt that her admission had been true, he still wasn't certain her passion for the vreal world platform he ruled was as steadfast and compassionate as she claimed. But if he wanted her help, she needed to understand what he knew.

"I've made a discovery inside Gaia, Johanna."

The way curiosity pushed wide her eyes suggested intrigue.

"Accidentally, but nonetheless. There's a path between it and the Kingdom. I think...I think whoever is attacking us from inside Gaia is getting to us from there."

Johanna clutched the gold chain at her throat. "That's impossible. They're two completely different systems with the highest security protocols in the industry."

"But they run on the same source code."

"Yes, but...Your Highness, that's just not how it works."

"Why wouldn't it? Even if it's true, as you say, that hackers have never managed to get into Gaia, I know some have gotten into the Kingdom through the years. Don't talk to me like I don't understand this stuff." Francisco shot to his feet, looking down at the woman. "You know who I am."

"Yes, Prince Francisco Batista de le Reina, grandson of Martin Batista de la Leon, the man who funded Omala Grover's first iteration of Gaia."

"You also know that I studied vreal design and architecture with some of the best teachers in the world, and I put myself through pirate port after pirate port to learn."

"You don't need to tell me." She traced a finger over the edge of her desk, following its path with her eyes. "The judge involved may have sealed your juvenile records, but I have access to all of our internal files. And while I can't share that information with anyone, as prescribed by law, I have read them. I know what you did. Or, should I say, *tried* to do to the Kingdom?"

At his sides, his fists clenched. "I didn't win my crown just because of my family connections. I have skills. Those, combined with the powers of my office... I could make life difficult for you, Johanna. I could make things for Plaxis very difficult."

"Do you think I'm your enemy?" Pursing her lips, her eyes rose to meet his. "I'm not, and I have just as much to lose if word gets around about these events as you do. The Kingdom is a network of powerful and affluential people, each of whom vie mightily for access. There have only been three successful hacks in fifteen years, and we've crushed them and patched the weaknesses they exposed *immediately*. Even still, our stock tanked each time it happened, and took months to recover. Gaia is built on the same security protocols and framework. If word gets out that someone's not only hacking into it, but destroying parts, it will ruin Plaxis."

Left hanging in the air between them: the destruction of Gaia, and all that implied. Francisco's hand absently went to his father's watch.

"Since you can't give me the source code, give me access to the Kingdom's user records. I'll figure out who would have motive and who might have the means to have discovered and exploited this hidden connection."

"Absolutely not," Johanna snapped. "Just because you're the sovereign of Gaia doesn't mean you have access to that kind of personal data for *our* clients. Frankly, *Frank*, I'm surprised someone with your reputation would even ask that. Or has your throne corrupted you so quickly?"

Now his teeth joined his fists, and Francisco's voice strained against the tension in his jaw. "The consequences if Gaia falls will extend far beyond some Saudi prince having his mask taken away."

"But what hope is there for Gaia if Plaxis is damaged by your actions?" "Our clients expect us to honor their privacy. Our product is one where they can act without judgement or reprimand. They perform acts inside they'd never dream of committing in the real, but that they wouldn't want getting out. You used to know that, or have you forgotten?" She turned her gaze to the city below their feet. "Before you tried to damage the Kingdom's infrastructure, you *committed* a few acts yourself. Attempted murder, if I recall."

"Attempted murder is a stretch. I just wanted him to suffer."

"Pity. If you had managed to kill Hugo Ferrente de Miguel, then one of Plaxis's biggest competitors never would have existed. Luckily, he's also one of my best customers. Likes to keep an eye on us, I guess."

The subtext of her comment, namely, *why wouldn't the man who took your real crown from you also come after your vreal one,* hit him, but Francisco let it go. He'd litigated that suspicion already. Hugo was scum, but he hadn't shown any hostility towards Gaia. As much as Francisco would like a reason to pursue the bastard, there just wasn't the grounds to do so.

He had to change tactics. This back and forth wasn't getting him anywhere. "The Gaia charter countersigned by Plaxis provides me with the right to a liaison. If you can't give me direct access to the user profiles, I at least demand you assign me someone who can comment on his or her observations inside the platform."

"Kaylie knows the ones who frequent the palace," she continued.

"I have complete access to all user profiles and make it a point to know everyone worth knowing."

"You really want me to spend time with your daughter." Francisco grinned as the image of a chess board overlaid the space between them in his mind's eye. Then, more to himself, he said aloud, "I wonder why."

Johanna smirked. "We are both royalty in our own way, and royals have been... *making alliances* of mutual benefit for eons."

Francisco leaned forward, running the middle finger of his right hand in a slow, laborious arc on Johanna's desk. "If the Gaian prince were to *enter* the Kingdom, would some be forthcoming? Letting me know who they truly are?"

"Particularly the young women, I'd imagine." Johanna suddenly came up to speed with where Francisco was heading, and the seduction play turned into fury. "Absolutely not! You think you can go into the Kingdom and lure the anarchists into the open? Do you want explosions going off in my palace, too? You can't squash those kinds of events there like you've been able to do with Gaia. Do you have any idea what that would do to our reputation?"

"Don't be silly, I don't want explosions," Francisco retorted. "The whole point of this is to end the violence going on in my capital. But to do that, I'm going to have to find the person hiding in yours."

"No one hides in my kingdom," Johanna said. "The consequences are too great."

"That's what I'm banking on." Francisco clapped as he rose to his feet. "Put out the word to your most prominent users, Tieg. The prince will be hosting a ball in three days at the palace, and he wants to party. It's time I reacquaint myself with who these 'Kingdom people' are. And it's time for them to understand the kind of man I've become."

SIXTEEN

WHEN SHE'D AWOKEN TO a talking mouse, Cindira considered that she might still be dreaming. Now, as she looked at the pair of transparent shoes in her hands and tried to believe they represented a nearly mythical high-tech device, the dream theory gained considerable traction.

"I don't understand." She held the right shoe to the light, seeing a clear, if slightly bent vision of the wall on the other side. "How could these possibly be jackpods? They look like a pair of sneakers and a shot glass had a crazy night together."

"Your mother preferred to call them slippers, miss." The mouse scurried up Cindira's sleeve, perching itself on her shoulder. "I think because she could use them to *slip* inside Gaia from anywhere. And, although you can't see it, there's circuitry a plenty in there. She managed to use…"

"Nanites." Cindira completed the mouse's sentence as the thought occurred to her in parallel. "But I thought research into them was abandoned years ago."

"Outlawed, actually."

She turned her eyes on the mouse, a difficult thing to do with him so close to her face. "These are illegal?"

"Only if anyone finds out about them."

Guilt gnawed at her, pushing her to admit that, in fact, someone *did* know about them. Luckily, Kaylie had dismissed the shoes as someone playing games, sending fakes copying some famous designer's work. If her stepsister had known they contained illegal technology, she certainly would have no hesitation in using it to her advantage.

Or taking them for herself.

"You must make sure to keep that from happening," Laporte continued. "Even your father was not fully aware of the extent of your mother's work in this area. It was privately funded, all research carried out in Europe."

"You're telling me my mom had a secret life."

"A *private life*, actually, though I know the concept of that seems an anathema in these times. Omala didn't believe anyone was entitled to anything in her head or her heart. You and I are the only ones she truly opened up with, and in both cases, with restrictions due to our particular shortcomings."

When Cindira's face fell, Laporte developed a humanlike ability to correct himself.

"That was a poor choice of words, madame. What I mean is, you were still a child when she died. In time, I'm certain she would have shared all her secrets with you, but of course you weren't ready back then. Likewise, while I retain the ability to understand and react to human emotions, at the end of the day, my capability as a confidante has its limits."

Like the slippers, this revelation bent the shape of her memories. Even though her mother had died while Cindira was in middle school, she still felt a kinship with the woman — uncommon for one of her age. It was almost as if the two were sisters rather than parent and child — though Omala could and did shift into an authoritarian role at will. Rarely. No, they had a comradery. Nevertheless, she'd always known there were things her mother kept hidden. Or perhaps better to say, *reserved*. Cindira had had no doubts that as she grew older, she too would be let into the fantastical worlds her mother walked, both in reality and vreality.

They'd simply never gotten the chance.

Cindira resumed her study of the silicone slippers. "I'm not even sure I need these. I was able to hack into Gaia simply enough."

"Technically, you didn't *hack* into anything. You logged into a parallel holding room for which you had anachronistic privileges and a waiting host profile."

Her heart quickened when she remembered that her mother's avatar still lay on that bed. "It's not gone, is it? Our apartment in Gaia?"

"No, madame, though I just stated, that apartment is not *in* Gaia." The mouse blinked a few times. "You used to be so much more able to follow these discussions. Your understanding of code and structure has diminished without my tutelage."

"You're very conceited for an AI entity." *But to stay on task...* "I get what you're saying, but what I'm getting at is, if these were designed for Gaia, what makes you think I'll be able to use them for the Kingdom?"

"Because the Kingdom is nothing more than Gaia's source code laced over far too many cosmetic layers. Your father and Johanna could never break into the source code themselves, but that didn't mean they couldn't make a clone of it. Probably they thought by putting it on servers that Omala didn't have access to, and instituting a new lattice of security measures, they could keep her out. They didn't realize that your mother had foreseen the possibility that someone might build another world without her authorization. She built doors into the source code. That same door your mother walked through to get into Gaia can just as easily walk into the Kingdom, or any other platform Plaxis creates using her work."

"A door that can open into both platforms?" She remembered watching the prince meander through her stepsister's vreal bedroom. "And are these shoes – the *slippers* – the only way to open that door?"

As much as the mouse could, he nodded. "The only way."

Well, there went that bubble of a theory.

But she wasn't going to think about it right now. No doubt the prince had resources aplenty, hackers and crackers, ways of getting around security measures. Right now, she needed to focus on the topic at hand. Or, Cindira thought as she looked at the slippers, at *feet*.

"How do they work?"

The mouse blinked twice. "You put them on."

"That's it?"

"No, but if you'll forgive the pun, that's the first step. And they must be worn without any interface. No socks, I'm afraid."

Just like the Indian-styled footwear her mother had preferred. Cindira laid the slippers on the floor and took a seat in preparation, pulling off her own everyday socks and shoes. "And after I put them on, do they turn on somehow? Do I have to voice-command them?"

"They wouldn't be a covert device if you had to noticeably interact with them."

"But you have to, you know..." With fingers spread wide, her hands mixed the air. "I mean, a jackpod is designed to be laid down in, in part for safety. Even though the neural interface reads and writes to the brain, the physical body occasionally moves in response to mental stimuli. I don't exactly remember my mother taking lots of naps."

"No, but she did daydream quite a bit, didn't she?"

No sooner had Cindira opened her mouth to argue the statement than a cascade of memories came down over her. That distant look her mother would often have, her quiet moments of passivity which Cindira wrote off as "deep thinking." Omala had been a genius, after all, and an innovative mind was given to wander. She knew this from personal experience.

"She was inside of Gaia?"

"Your mother had a few secure points of entry in various locations around the platform," Laporte acknowledged. "Ones that were hidden from view and let her peak in for a few moments at a time when she wanted—or needed—to."

"But what about her avatar?" Cindira asked. "How did she show up at a specific location if her avatar is in our apartment even now?"

"An avatar is nothing but code, and even a world as complex as Gaia, nothing more than a vast array of programming and algorithms. For most users, the avatars are put away in a VR equivalent of a file. But your mother's avatar was stored at the root directory. It meant she could drill down anywhere she wanted. In time, you may learn to do the same." Laporte's head tilted to the side. "While the topic has been breached, madame, can we discuss the destruction of your childhood avatar in the explosion?"

"Not really sure there's much to discuss. It was there, now it's not. Probably just as well, since I'm twenty-six, and it was still eleven."

"Be that as it may, it leaves you without a place to land when you try to jack in. We'll need to design you a new avatar, and soon. There are things going on inside that I'm having a hard time accounting for. Things which may make better sense to human eyes."

She put the slippers down and stood. "If it's an avatar I need, I'm going to have to go to Plaxis. I don't have resources to create that here."

Which begged the question, where had her mother done all this stuff? Laporte had mentioned an off-grid lab? When she'd turned twenty-one, all of her mother's papers and belongings, held in trust by her father, reverted to her. There wasn't much to it all—especially not after fifteen years in the proxy possession of Johanna Tieg. Most of the money was gone. Had probably been the first thing to go. A few dozen boxes of household and personal affects still sat in a storage locker in Oakland. She'd gone through it once but didn't recall coming across anything suggesting a clandestine life her mother her led under everyone's nose.

All things she'd need to bring up and discuss with Laporte, once she knew that she could trust him.

And that she wasn't, in fact, dreaming all this.

"I'd suggest waiting until you'd normally attend to your duties there; with your recent actions, if a spotlight catches a toe, they'll want to illuminate the whole body of your activities. Don't do anything outside your normal routine. As your friend Scotia would say, 'act cool.'"

Her eyebrow shot up. "You know Scotia?"

"I know *of* Scotia. I've attended several of her lectures on vreal addiction and treatment. She truly is a gifted researcher with a true passion for helping the afflicted."

The much was true, but it sounded as though the mouse had an opinion. That was odd for an AI entity.

"Fine," Cindira huffed. "I'll wait until my shift tomorrow to do anything. And what about you? Are you, like, my little sidekick now?"

"I'd prefer to think that I am assuming the place in your life I once held for your mother. I am your spy, as well as your assistant. Unless you'd prefer otherwise, I'd like to accompany you. But if I may ask one accommodation?"

Cindira dipped her chin. "Sure, what?"

"That you hide Asla's broom. She's nearly smashed me twice."

SEVENTEEN

SHE WISHED THERE WAS another place that she could handle this kind of work. Any kind of work. Humility was for the forgotten; Cindira knew she was the best coder the company had. One of the best in the world, frankly. But her talents were useless without the tools to practice them, and Plaxis held control over them all. It was like being a master sculptor, but without access to clay and marble.

Hiding her new project, a brand-new avatar for herself, from her coworkers had been simple enough. It wasn't the first time she'd undertaken building a profile from scratch; her superior coding skills meant Johanna often assigned Cindira the task for the clients who agreed to pay the hefty fees (not that Cindira herself ever saw an additional cent for her labor or any form of recognition.) The others were busy with assignments of their own and didn't notice the meek woman on Cindira's screen had begun to look more like a reflection than a rendition.

Generally, only celebrities whose brand was heavily tied up in their image designed avatars identical to their real-world selves, and Cindira was hardly a celebrity. A fleeting thought dashed across her mind: Her real-world self was her avatar. *This* couldn't possibly be her true self.

"Oh, good, you're here."

Cindira blacked out the screen at her workstation as Kaylie unexpectantly entered the Kitchens and lingered at the corner of her desk. *Act cool*, she inwardly lectured.

"I do work here, Kaylie."

Frustration made her snippy, it seemed. She'd had so little experience with it, and Kaylie even less with being on the receiving end, that it made both women pause and take on awkward expressions.

Kaylie blinked away hers first. "Yeah, well, anyway... Stop whatever it is you're doing. I need a new dress."

Cindira pointed back over her shoulder. "I saw a sale at McCarran's on my way in."

"What? No, not a dress! I mean a *dress dress*, for the Kingdom!"

"Another one?" Was the previous week set on replay? "I just made you one, then tweaked it even more."

"Right, and now I need another one."

Even for Kaylie, two custom-made dresses in as many weeks seemed excessive. "Why so soon? I'm sure there's still plenty of men who haven't seen you out of the other one."

Kaylie ate the insult with a great deal of effort. "There's a ball, and I need a new gown."

"There's a ball every night in the Kingdom."

"Yes, but not ones attended by the prince."

"The prince?" That got her attention. "The Gaian prince?"

Kaylie rolled her eyes. "What other prince do you know?"

"There's one in the Nordic Triumvirate, Catalonia, Japan... I think the Saudis have several dozen, and—"

"Yes, the Gaian prince!" Kaylie snapped. When her outburst drew the gazes of the other workers in the room, she brought herself back under control, though her words picked up speed and gruffness as she continued. "Prince Francisco has decided to reach out to the members of the Kingdom community to increase awareness of opportunities available to the wealthy to help the poor and destitute nations of the world, the ones who count on Gaia to mediate their problems. He's going to host a ball at the palace tomorrow night and everyone important is invited."

A throbbing tick started to increase in both tempo and volume. After a few moments, Cindira realized it was her own pulse pounding in her ears. So, the prince was holding a ball. But why would such a high-profile personality jump into a platform known as a scandalous playground of the rich and famous? And how had he gotten into Kaylie's room? If she was going to figure out what he was up to, she needed to be where he was.

"I want to go."

"You want to..." Kaylie threw back her head and laughed. "*You*, at the prince's ball? Don't be silly. You don't even have an avatar. What are you going to do, craft a whole new profile overnight? Please,

Cindira, the process takes days!"

Not if you know Purusha Prime and your name is Cindira Tieg. "It wouldn't take too long if I just used a digital scan of myself as a template. It wouldn't have to be anything fancy."

"Yes, it would," Kaylie insisted. "Eloquence—or *fancy,* as you call it—is part of our branding for that platform. It's all about the luxe, the fairytale, the overly-romanticized idea of a world of wonder and magic. You can't go into the Kingdom with some half-baked avatar, glitching all over the place and disgusting users who pay through the nose for exclusive access! It's an idealized landscape, Cindira, not a horror flicker simulation! Besides, if you spend all your time scrapping together a new avatar from scratch before tomorrow night, then who would make my dress?"

"Any number of etailors." She didn't mean for the answer to sound snippy, but it was hard to fold it into any other shape. Like it or not, she'd never be able to make herself an avatar without Plaxis's resources, and Kaylie was now her boss. When Kaylie shot daggers at her, Cindira found herself crumbling. "Fine, you're right. I just...I dreamed for a moment."

Kaylie savored the taste of her small victory, grinning. "I thought I had finally cured you of that habit."

Sometimes I wonder. "What color do you want?"

"Blue for me. Mother wants dark purple, and Cade would like you to design a suit for him that compliments both."

Cindira's eyes went wide. "*Three* new projects by tomorrow afternoon?"

"By tomorrow *morning,*" Kaylie amended. "We'll need a chance to try them on and make any adjustments before we leave for the ball."

It might as well be three hundred. "I'm good, Kaylie, but I'm not that good. You...I couldn't possibly make three new projects from scratch in twenty-four hours."

And have any hope of fixing up an avatar for myself.

"Do, or don't. Your choice. But an employee who can't meet deadlines might not have a job if she fails to meet them."

Cindira leaned back. "This isn't part of my job."

"Isn't it?" Kaylie sneered. "Are you not the lead code writer on the customization division? Are you not receiving a direct order from your supervisor?"

"But, Kaylie, I—"

"Enough!" The blonde clapped her hands in Cindira's face, cutting off her words. "Mother, Cade, and I will meet you tomorrow in the Sink to inspect your work. Now, get busy."

Cindira collapsed back into her chair in the wake of Kaylie's departure, her forehead falling against fingertips pressed into her temples. Never mind the fact that she herself was going to miss the ball, the perfect opportunity to get close to the prince without any of his usual security detail and figure out what was really going on inside of Gaia. Now, on top of that, she'd be working overnight just to get the clothing programmed.

She stirred when she felt a hand on her shoulder. Cindira turned her head up to find that one of her junior coders, a mousy woman whose name she couldn't recall, staring down at her with a tender smile. Behind her, the dozen other coders on duty flanked her.

"Don't worry, Miss Tieg," the soft voice cooed. "We'll help you."

EIGHTEEN

KAYLIE STRODE INTO view, her gown so diaphanous, its voluminous ivory skirting made her appear to be walking through rolling mist. Such had been the intention of the design, and to Cindira's delight, her vision had been realized.

Just because she didn't want the work didn't mean she couldn't take pride in it.

Her stepsister extended an arm, examining the complex silver stitchery on her sleeve. "You're certain this wasn't just pulled out of some old file? Seems very detailed for something thrown together in a day."

Cindira labored to suppress her ire as she pushed the button on the control panel that let her voice be heard in Kaylie's vreal bedroom. "Every single thread is newly programmed. I've cross-referenced against all the other gowns that have been uploaded to client libraries in the last three days since the ball was announced. This dress is by far the most elegant and the most complex."

"And the color?" Kaylie smoothed her hands over the bodice. "Didn't I tell you that I wanted blue? I've never worn white in the Kingdom before. Does it suit me?"

Nearby, Mackey fixed a hungry gaze on the boss lady. "I'll say."

"Shhh!" Cindira pressed a finger to a smile she couldn't hide. As soon as the others quieted their own giggles, she opened the channel again. "It's not white precisely." *It would be misadvertising if I put you in something suggesting you were pure.* "It has a tinge of blue in it, enough to shade it. The Kingdom's lighting algorithms don't treat pure white well. It confuses it for translucent, and I've even heard reports that sometimes it looks like the user's clothing disappears."

A wily, cocky half-grin pulled up a corner of Kaylie's mouth. "That doesn't sound like an entirely unwelcome glitch, but not right for tonight."

Time for the upsell. The last thing Cindira wanted to admit to was that she and the other coders had decided a mostly monochromatic palette would make their jobs easier. Color created complexity. "I modeled your dress after old videos of the marine layer. You will *roll* into the room, blanketing out everything else so that the only thing anyone sees when they turn in any direction is your presence."

"And I'll leave them feeling wet."

Cindira bit her tongue on that.

"So...?" She drew out the word and her hopes, waiting for judgement.

Kaylie huffed and let her arms fall to the side. "It will do, I suppose."

Cindira's hope for even the slightest bit of appreciation evaporated.

Kaylie appeared to be looking right at them, even though it was impossible for her to see the Kitchens from inside the Kingdom. "You're going to turn off this mirror contraption when I leave, right? I don't want any of you spying into my bedroom later. I *may not* be alone."

In her own bedroom? Whenever Kaylie had undertaken one of her virtual hookups before, it was outside of Alsace. *Not* that the two women shared intimate details of their love lives, or if they had, that Cindira would have had much to share. The men in whom Kaylie took interest were wealthy enough to have their own mansions, and going to their place was easier and safer than having Cindira upgrade the security setting on the profile of her *beau du jour.* Not to mention, she shared the space with her mother and brother. Even inside virtual reality, how creepy would that be? That Kaylie planned to have a guest without such concerns meant only one thing.

"You've already given the prince security clearance for Alsace?" Cindira asked.

"Of course, I did," Kaylie snipped back. "He doesn't use the royal residence made available for his office here in the Kingdom. The only place for me to have him would be for him to *come* here."

Kaylie Fife rarely let an entendre go undoubled.

Cindira pushed the mic button again. "Aren't you scared you'll be interrupted?"

The fact that Kaylie didn't answer told Cindira all she needed to know. This wasn't just another virtual conquest for Kaylie. This plan had larger implications, ones that, no doubt, Johanna was part of.

But those all depended on the prince buying in, and that he'd be into someone like Kaylie. The flirtation His Highness had shown during his visit as Detective Batista fled the moment he understood Kaylie couldn't give him what he was after. Who was to say that hadn't changed though?

In the back of her mind, Cindira wondered what the prince would make of a quiet, brainy girl instead.

"We'll shut down the window right after you leave. I'm the only one from the Kitchens who has clearance to enter Alsace, and I won't be here much longer."

A smile teased Cindira's voice.

"Cade and my mother say they find their outfits acceptable, so I suppose we're done here. Close the window." Kaylie grabbed a matching handbag off the table next to her. "I'm off to the ball."

No sooner had Kaylie stepped out of view and presumably, left the room, than Cindira whipped around to her team. They deserved her praise. They deserved her thanks. They deserved her appreciation and recognition. They deserved a bottle of wine and the rest of the night off.

All things she'd have to give them later.

"I really hate to do this, but I have to go."

NINETEEN

"I STILL DON'T HAVE an avatar." Cindira slung her backpack over her shoulder as she shot out of the Kitchens. "Not sure how I'm pulling this off without one."

Laporte emerged from his hiding spot, a zippered pocket on the front of the bag, and crawled up to perch upon Cindira's shoulder. "You *do* have one you can use still."

"No, it was destroyed in an explosion, remember?" *Though even if it hadn't, wouldn't it freak out Batista to see me approaching him after I blew up in front of him?* "I'd barely gotten the wireframes on the replacement drawn yesterday when Kaylie came in about her stupid dress."

"It was a beautiful dress, though, madame."

"You have to stop calling me 'madame,' Laporte."

"Yes, miss."

Miss? At least it didn't make her feel like a brothel owner.

The mouse continued. "When she diverted you from your task, I was forced to find a solution."

Cindira stopped dead in her tracks. "What? How?"

"I took the liberty of preparing a render very similar to your real-world representation." He kept silent for a moment, except that so close to her ear, Cindira swore there was some sort of high-pitched tone coming from inside of it. "Your family has left Alsace. It is now safe for you to use it is a port entry undetected."

"I wish there was a better place to get in."

"As you yourself have said, it's the only port of entry in the area which won't trigger an arrival record. Ideally, you'd enter through the magic pumpkin, but as I've noted, *its* entrance point to the Kingdom is very far from the palace."

"Couldn't you just edit the entry logs?" She reached the room she'd been heading for, the only one she could think of where no one would come in to find her. Not even the custodian had access to Kaylie's new office. Cleaning staff were only allowed in with the division head present. Cindira had been granted access by Kaylie herself, "just in case I ever need you to do something for me when I'm not here."

"I have access to the source code, miss, but all the structure that Plaxis has built into the Kingdom since its inception is beyond my influence. I can only read the files, not overwrite them."

After fifteen years, Cindira had discovered the first flaw in her mother's work. She ducked into the office, locking the door behind her before throwing her bag on Kaylie's desk. Inside, the silicone slippers sat, wrapped inside a gym towel. It was the only thing she could see when she'd looked around her room that she was sure no one would want to examine too closely. She wasn't sure *why* anyone would be rifling through her bag to begin with, but she'd never had anything with so much value to be found before. It was doing things to her head.

"That's hard to believe. I can change the records easily."

The mouse's nose twitched. "Then why don't you, miss?"

"Because I'm not allowed to."

"You did it when you and Miss MacAvoy were running away from the Stadium that one night."

How did Laporte know about that? "That was different. That was for a system outside of Plaxis. My contract says I can't alter UX/UA records here without a direct sign off from a supervisor or court order."

If it was possible for a botic to look disappointed, Laporte did. "That's too bad."

Was that some form of passive aggressive goading? Whatever, she didn't have time to delve into her prepared lists of reasons she never wanted to do anything that brought the wrong kind of atten-tion. Cindira set the slippers on the floor, aligning them with her feet before slipping her shoes and socks off and stuffing them in the bag. "You said it's best if I lay down until I get used to using them, just in case. I guess I can do that here on the floor, but are you sure this isn't going to, like, fry my brain?"

"No, it will not 'fry your brain.'" The mouse's tone managed to be mocking despite its inability to have true emotions. "Once you put them on, they will need about thirty seconds to boot up and acclimate to your neural signals."

"They read my brain waves through the soles of my feet? Is it safe? Is it painful?"

"I assure you, it's safe. I will send the command for the devices to jack you into the Kingdom when you're ready. Remember the sensation. Everything your body experiences is the result of chemical and electrical impulses. After this first time, you should be able to jack in on your own whenever you wish by clearly recalling the experience you're about to have. It's a kind of macro command."

Cindira fixed the slippers in her gaze, then looked at her bare feet, then the slippers again. Either she was going to do this, or she wasn't.

She drew in a breath, closed her eyes, and lifted her right foot.

And then came the knock on the door.

Three quick taps sent her pulse spiraling as Laporte turned towards the entry.

"Speaking of Miss MacAvoy, I believe that must be her."

"Oh my god, the invitation!" Cindira ignored the shoes and rushed to the other side of the room. "I almost forgot."

Laporte had scrambled out of view by the time Cindira had collected herself enough to open the door. When she did, it was only to crack it wide enough to press her face into view.

"Scotia, thank you for coming."

The redhead narrowed her gaze, suspicion taking hold of her features. "What's going on? Why am I meeting you at Kaylie's office, and why aren't you opening the door?" She curled up on her tippy toes, trying to see over her friend's head. "What are you hiding in there?"

"Why would you think I'm trying to hide something?"

"Because you won't let me see inside?" The redhead fell back to her heels and cocked a hip. "What's up with you? You show up at my house in the middle of the night after saying you'd blown up the Prince of Gaia, and disappear the morning after without so much as a goodbye. Then, I don't hear from you until this morning when you send a message begging to use my invitation to the Ball."

"You didn't want to go anyway. Cade only gave you the invitation so he could hit on you when he's a little better looking to the eye."

Her stepbrother hadn't been blessed by genetics the way Kaylie had and didn't seem interested in any kind of cosmetic surgery to change it. *Men don't have to be good looking to get women,* Cindira had overheard him say once during a rare family dinner. *It's our power and our money women want. Why would I slice myself up when I already have both of those things?*

"I *had* thought about going actually," Scotia snapped back. "Just because Cade thinks he can woo me by inviting me to this fancy royal ball thing doesn't mean I wouldn't go just to spite him. The annual St. Dymphna's fundraiser is coming up, and I could have used it as an opportunity to coerce some early donations, maybe even a sponsorship or two. Don't be so presumptive."

Cindira felt like she'd drunk a cup of vinegar. "You're right, I am being presumptive, and I'm sorry. I'm also sorry for the way I've been acting lately. I promise, I'll make it up to you. And I swear, I'm not trying to keep something from you, but for the moment, I have to. It has... *had* something to do with my mom."

All true, and all things she didn't have time to go into further at the moment.

"Do you have the invitation?"

Scotia raised her comque and clicked a few screens. Soon enough, the projection of a rectangular invite inscribed in archaic artist script hovered a few inches above her wrist. "You do realize all the credentials went out yesterday, and if you didn't RSVP by this morning, the invitation was revoked."

"I can alter the coding to change that. It just has to scan as valid when I enter the palace."

"It won't do any good," Scotia argued. "If the credential doesn't match your profile when midnight hits, you're still going to be kicked out."

"That's more than enough time."

Scotia grimaced. "To do what?"

Cindira bit her bottom lip, a series of consequences spinning in her mind. None of the possible results seemed worse than lying to her best friend. "It's the only way I can think of to talk to the prince."

"The prince?" Scotia repeated. "Why would you need to talk to him? Is it about what happened when you were inside Gaia? Hey, didn't you say your avatar was destroyed? Did you make... Where are you going?"

Cindira looked past her guilt to remember the truth: she was stepping into risky territory, and any knowledge she gave her best friend would only place her in danger.

"I'm sorry, Scotia, I really am. But I can't tell you anymore. Thank you for giving me your invitation. Thank you for *everything,* but I really have to go."

With the door locked and without any further delay, Cindira pulled the silicone slippers on to her bare feet. If she had been expecting anything miraculous to happen from that fact alone, she was severely disappointed. The only novel exception was that she now knew from experience that slippers made of silicone and with thousands of nanobots and microcircuitry woven into them were as comfortable as they sounded. Namely, not.

She laid back on the floor. "Now what?"

Laporte laid down by her right hand. "Just close your eyes and dream."

TWENTY

THE SUNSET CONSUMED the horizon, painting it in extravagant reds bursting with orange hues. Brilliant, blinding colors danced across her eyelids, burning her retinas with the most delicious tease. Cindira blinked, sitting up, taking her first look at a world her mother had unwittingly created. The light broke in from a square-paned window, and even as she sat up, the angle of the sunbeam pitched as the sun set outside. She was in Alsace, her stepmother's home inside the Kingdom. In the front parlor, from what she could tell. The plush fabric of the Persian rug beneath her felt so real as she pushed herself up to a seated position. The full-immersion experience proved much richer than just tinkering in the Sink.

Only then did she become aware of the stiff, itchy fabric scratching her legs.

"What am I wearing?"

The unflattering skirt looked more like an oversized towel she'd wrapped around and tucked at the waist. It came down to her ankles; a starched, white pinafore stretched nearly as far. The billowing blouse appeared to be made of gingerbread-colored gingham. On her head, white linen that came together in under her chin and melded seamlessly into a long collar that covered her chest, shoulders, and upper back. A veil? A nun's habit? She couldn't remember anyone saying the prince's ball would be a masquerade.

Cindira inspected herself with concern and curiosity. There was a bit of double vision going on, a phenomenon she'd forgotten in her years away from the vreal. It was like she was seeing two layers atop each other. On one, the surface: the rendering and manifestation of the underlayer. On that one, bits of code lined up and marched to a set of instructions, weaving and bobbing to execute.

Luckily, when she relaxed her eyes, Cindira saw only the surface like anyone else who might jack into the platform. Unluckily, what she saw on the surface in this moment was hardly pleasing.

"This isn't a ballgown."

Something had happened to her voice. It held a bit of an accent, perhaps? Which, she couldn't quite place, but something about it proved familiar, comforting. *Part of the fantasy*, she thought. Whatever made the world more enticing, thus, more addicting, Plaxis labored to achieve.

"Your task is better achieved by avoiding notice rather than drawing it." Laporte sounded like it was right next to her, though she couldn't see it anywhere. "I know we had discussed choosing a random dress from those in the Kingdom libraries left unused tonight, but I thought I might first present my argument for donning a servant's garb instead."

She smoothed her hands over the hem work of the simple garment. "If the point is to avoid attention, then I should be in a gown. I'm going to stand out dressed like this."

She stood, and immediately stopped in place. It wasn't that the costume was uncomfortable, even if a little over done with the weight of the cloth. It was that her shoes *clunked* when she walked.

Cindira pulled up the skirt and discovered why. In terms of shape, there was nothing unusual about her footwear. A gentle, wide-base heel and an elegant cut, they bore a similarity to the ones her mother used to like to wear under her fancier lehenga dresses whenever she was off to some fancy soiree. Only instead of leather or even woven cloth, her shoes appeared to be made of glass.

"What the heck is this?"

"A design flaw, miss," the still non-corporeal mouse said. "Or at least, a misjudgment, if I could be so bold as to make that statement. Your mother was brilliant, but even she made mistakes. While one is jacked into the vreal wearing the slippers, they will also render on the avatar once logged in. I apologize there is nothing to be done for it. I think your mother may have intended it to be some sort of indication of authority. If so, she never shared it with me."

The coder took a few steps to test their feel. "They're not as awkward here as they are in the real, but still..."

"You can change the shape later if you like. Although they appear to be glass, they won't break, and you'll find they're comfortable enough. For now, I can mute the code which causes them to make so much noise."

She tested that statement, tapping her foot a few times. Sure enough, the clink she might have expected failed to manifest.

"Good. If the goal is not to be noticed, sounding like I'm toasting everyone in the room every time I take a step would have made that difficult."

Cindira adjusted the pinafore and set about examining her own build, holding her arms before her and turning them over slowly. She couldn't detect any pixilation, and the contours of her form had been well and realistically rendered. As she looked down at herself, she slid her hand over the rise of her hip bone. *Exceptionally well rendered*, she thought.

"Where did the design for this outfit come from?"

Still no body, only Laporte's voice. "It is the design worn by the NPC servants in the palace."

"The Non-Player Characters?" Cindira asked, performing a little QA of her own. "We call those VAPORs now." She pressed an index finger to the patch of skin between her eyes, finding that Laporte had given her a fake bhindi. "I'm not sure I can pass as a VAPOR even with this marking. Surely someone will realize when they look at me that my eyes aren't a solid color and I don't move in that overly-responsive way that they do."

"That's the key to it, miss. In the palace, very few users ever even notice an NPC—a VAPOR, if you prefer. That includes your stepmother and siblings."

Arrogance was its own kind of blindness, she supposed. "How can we get to the palace?"

"By coach. One is on its way now; it will meet us out in the main street in a few minutes. The credential Scotia transferred to you will get you onto the palace grounds. However, as Scotia herself mentioned, the midnight protocols will sweep you out when it sees you and has no record of your entry."

"I know. Only, if that's true, how does my family get away with it?" She broadened her search around the first floor, looking to see in which corner the little mouse had stuffed himself. "*Why* are you hiding?"

"I'm not hiding, miss. I'm just... Well..." Its hesitance suggested contemplation, an internal debate. But that was impossible, wasn't it? Sure, Laporte's programming might encourage it to give emotional indicators, but it was just that... programming.

Finally, Laporte continued. "In the real, your mother decided to make me look like a mouse because rodents are both innocuous and pests. No one would hesitate to swat me away, as Asla has demonstrated. It also made my physical iteration very transportable. In the vreal, however, there is no need for such considerations. Just remember that I can look like anything you want except a registered avatar, so if my current appearance doesn't suit, I can alter it."

"You mean you look different here?"

But why shouldn't it be so? After all, the vast majority of Kingdom clients had avatars carefully tailored to be their ideal selves, whether that was getting rid of a bump on the nose, or by appearing slender and tone when the reality was anything but. Her stepsister had uncharacteristically gone against the trend. Kaylie's mods were skin deep. Literally. All her alterations had been performed in the real; why change in the vreal one that had so perfectly been rendered in flesh? Not to mention, Kaylie had been a public figure since not long after the Kingdom launched. Her stepsister must have felt her face was already part of her brand, and thus her appeal.

Laporte didn't speak. Instead, the doorknob of a nearby closet turned and the door creaked open.

As a human, Laporte was utterly unremarkable, and even retained some of his mousier qualities. Although he appeared as a boy in his late teens or early twenties, he was of a diminutive stature, the top of his head on par with her chin. Black hair, black eyes, an unassuming boyish smile. In every way plain and by that virtue, non-threatening.

"Is this iteration to your satisfaction?" The voice was the same, however.

Cindira smiled and nodded. "Why wouldn't it be? Is this avatar modeled on someone from the real?"

"It is, miss, though no one you ever had the opportunity to meet. He died when you were still a young child."

She put her hand to his cheek, examining his high cheek bones.

"It's funny. You're a botic, and I'd just gotten used to thinking of you as an *it*. Now I have to reframe my understanding of you."

"In the real, I feel like an it. My existence there is very utilitarian. But here..." He held his hands out to the side, as if to say, *look at me*. "This is as close as I come to feeling real. And if it would not be objectionable to you, in the vreal, I prefer to be addressed as *Mister* Laporte."

"Of course, *Mr. Laporte*."

The little mouse... No, the *man*, beamed. "Thank you, miss." Suddenly, he clapped his hands, making her jolt. "Enough. We mustn't waste time." He reached out and took her hand, pulling her toward the door. "The ball has already begun, and Yuchi will be suspicious if you arrive too late."

She let out a yelp as the mouse-turned-pageboy yanked on her arm a little too hard. Not that he could injure her, of course. One could experience pain inside the vreal; it was neural feedback deemed necessary to render the experience authentic, but death, when it rarely occurred, was merely symbolic.

Laporte pasted on an apologetic smile. "Sorry, Miss Cindira."

"No harm done." They made it out the front door. "Who is Yuchi?"

"The security bot that guards the palace."

In her mind, she visualized a sweet little Japanese woman well matched to the name, and the horrific yet funny prospect of watching such a woman dispense of trespassers.

"Only a certain level of paid clientele is permitted to enter," Laporte continued, "and tonight, those restrictions are even tighter. Yuchi makes sure that only those who are meant to be there, are there."

"Scotia's clearance is that high?"

Even from the side, she caught the young man's smile. "To be honest, I'm not certain if Miss MacAvoy is aware she's at such a high tier. The change to her profile was only recently requested by your brother, Cade."

"My *stepbrother*, you mean. And that explains it."

How could Cade get into Scotia's pants if Scotia couldn't get into Cade's ball? It was so pitiful. Didn't Cade know that Scotia was universes outside his league? Whatever. She couldn't focus on that now.

She needed to keep her mind on the obstacles to her goals.

"Is it Yuchi that executes the midnight protocols?"

"Indeed, and I'm not too eager to get on his bad side."

Well, perhaps she should have imagined a little Japanese *man*.

TWENTY-ONE

CINDIRA HAD SEEN SLIPS of the Kingdom before, even recognized passing elements of it as her own creation. But now, she could appreciate it in full. Here a flower in front of one of the luxurious mansions along the river, a combination of a red rose and a black tulip that held the petals of both. There a store front selling linens and dinnerware. (After all, if you were going to allow users to buy luxurious properties, they needed to furnish and decorate them.) But to see it with her own eyes! Or at least, eyes that belonged to her. It was as though someone had hooked a 3D printer into her dreams and manufactured her visions in real time. Depth, texture... even the scent of roasting hazelnuts in the air had all her senses buzzing. The streets weren't empty, either. They bustled, full of women and men strolling, dressed in varying levels of baroque finery. There were even a few dogs and one man walking a monkey on a leash. Bots, of course. One couldn't jack a real animal into the vreal; they didn't have the cerebral capacity for it.

Cindira wanted to order the coach to stop so she could get out and explore each inch in excruciating detail. Beside her on the bench sat Laporte, diminutive in stature and miniscule in interest about all they were passing.

He fished a piece of gold-leafed card stock from his pocket and handed it to her. "Here. This is the invitation Scotia transferred to you. I've rewritten the code to timestamp it as verified yesterday."

Her fingers indexed the bumps and crevices of the fine parchment, marveling in the experience. "It feels so real. How will this get me through? Yuchi will take one look at me dressed as a servant and know that something is wrong."

"The invitation itself is the key. You perceive it as paper, but all this really represents is a package of code, credentials."

She tucked the card into a pocket in her skirt. "You must know every inch of this place after so many years, but how much can you see beyond the avatars and objects? How deep does your knowledge go? Do you know where everyone is?"

The young man clicked his tongue. "I know who is signed in; when they pass into a new section of the program, I know that they are in *that* area. I don't know specifics beyond that. For example, I can tell you the prince, as well as your family, are currently in the palace. But where in the palace precisely? I don't know. To me, that information all looks the same."

A glimmer of an idea crept into the back of her brain. Maybe she wouldn't have to track down Batista at all. Maybe Laporte could simply tell her what she needed to know. "When someone's logged in, can you read their mind?"

Wide-eyed, the mouse-turned-man looked aghast. "Of course not. Your mother was adamant in my design and in the design of her platform that the user's mind would remain free of intrusion any more than was necessary to control its avatar. A wise human once said, 'knowledge is power.' Omala understood that and knew the first temptation of a creation such as hers would be to use it as a mechanism of intelligence. How would Gaia have saved the world, if it was simultaneously building the chains that would enslave it?"

For reasons she couldn't quite vocalize, Cindira felt ashamed of even asking. Before she could continue the topic, however, the road under the wheels of the coach turned from dirt to cobblestone, making their smooth ride into a bumpy, jostling nightmare.

"We've entered the palace grounds," Laporte said to her unasked question.

She slipped her hand into her pocket. The air rushed from her chest when she found it empty. "The invitation...it disappeared!"

"But you did not." He smiled as the coach began to slow and the discomfort abated. "That means it—and you—have been given a pass by Yuchi. The first hurdle is crossed."

Cindira pulled herself to the edge of the bench, peaking her head past the heavy curtained window just in time to see the backside of the palace gates. The archway was truly a marvel to behold. She'd read articles about it in VR architectural reviews, and knew it was modeled after the Habsburg Gate in the real with one significant difference: the massive clock face set in the top of the arch. One of the early challenges in a VR environment had been deciding how time would work, and if there should be time at all. Cindira's mother had argued it was a constant in the real world, and in the virtual one, a human mind would falter without it. Unlike Gaia, the Kingdom moved in time with +0 GMT. The Baum Clock at the palace measured time with computer precision, running eight hours ahead of San Francisco.

Cindira eased back into her seat. "What's the next hurdle?"

"Surviving long enough to find the prince."

The coach pulled to a stop at the back of the grounds. Laporte presented a hand, helping Cindira to step down safely, before ushering her into a room where a staff of several dozen worked a kitchen that looked like something from a period piece movie. All around, women dressed in identical wear went about their business. For a moment, Cindira worried they'd see her classifiers – her servant's garb—and assume she was one of them. To her surprise, however, none of them paid her the slightest mind.

"Are they all bots?"

Laporte surveyed the servants, then pointed to one man working at a distant table, folding pieces of pastry into edible origami. "The sous chef is from the real. Bots can mix consistent, delicious recipes, but only a true chef can give them a human touch. In essence, he's here to make the meal perfect, by making it slightly *imperfect.*"

"That's a contradiction."

"That's humanity," Laporte shot back.

No one took notice of them as they passed, a fact that both relieved and confused her. How far would she be able to make it into the palace without the security bots realizing she wasn't who the invitation said she was? After a few minutes weaving through halls, the level of opulence rising with each turn like a set of river locks slowly filling and carrying the boat within higher, they came to a circular vestibule where three intimating oak doors stretched from floorboards to crown molding.

"This is one of the pipelines," Laporte said, and as he continued he held up a hand to indicate each in turn from left to right. "The backroom, only accessible by décor bots and a limited number of Plaxis avatars. When the Kingdom was being constructed without Omala's knowledge, it was from this point forward. The center door leads to the residential part of the palace, though no one really lives here. It's called the Coeur. High-end users can rent out that portion for exorbitant fees, but only on a nightly basis. Think of it as a luxurious bordello. *They* do."

Her stomach curdled as she thought of the difference between all the good Gaia did, and all the malicious, indulgent activities that kept the Kingdom ticking.

Finally, Laporte extended a pointed finger to the last door. "That way eventually leads to the ballroom, and also the library, the dining rooms, the throne room, and eventually, the terraces and drives that connect the palace with the rest of the kingdom. If you're looking for the prince, that is likely where you'll find him."

"But it's also where my family will be. I don't want Kaylie or Johanna to know I'm here. I hope you're right, that I blend in as a servant, but if they look straight at me, they're going to realize who I am."

"That's highly unlikely."

"Yeah, well, I wish I had your confidence." Cindira looked at each of the doors in turn. "If only there were a way for me to look for the prince without being in the room. God, I wish this world had electronics. I'd march a drone bug in there without thinking."

Laporte took in her side profile. "Miss Cindira, may I ask what it is you're hoping to accomplish here tonight?"

He asked the question like an AI entity would: simply, and as though the answer should be equally as simple. But like Laporte himself had said, humans were perfectly imperfect.

"I need to talk to the prince."

"To what end?"

Wasn't that the question? "I don't know if I can put it into words yet. Explosions in the Gaian capital being covered up? The prince sniffing around at Plaxis? I need to know what's going on, if my mother's legacy is truly in danger. I know you don't understand what instinct is..."

"Instinct: noun. An innate, typically fixed pattern of behavior in animals in response to certain stimuli."

"Yes, but do you *understand* it? The prince feels like the way to fight whatever is going on in Gaia is by having access to the source code." She shook her head, as though she could shake away the fuzziness of what she was thinking. "Maybe it's as simple as the code breaking down after years of use without proper updates. I've been trying to patch it, but I'm doing it blind. I shouldn't have stayed gone for so long, not if I was going to keep working at Plaxis. It would have been different if I just walked away from vreality altogether, but I didn't. Now, I need to understand. What's going on, and why is the prince trying to pry? Especially since I'm the only one who..."

The mouse looked at her with his human eyes full of hope. "You're the only one who can help." As suddenly as his pride had come over him, he masked it with reproach. "A fact that makes you the most dangerous person in the Kingdom."

"How?"

"Miss Tieg, you seem to be under the impression that Gaia is the platform which serves as the world's place for diplomacy and war-craft. It is the public face, I'll grant you that. But what you—and based on what you're saying, perhaps Prince Francisco—need to realize is that *this world* is where the money and power truly are. And they are growing weary of competition."

He pulled her towards the center door, which opened as though by magic upon their approach. "Come, there is one room in the res-idence from which you can see the ballroom below. Don't worry, it doesn't work the other way. You'll be safely hidden, and from there, you can get the full picture of what's really going on."

TWENY-TWO

KAYLIE FIFE WAS IN her natural habitat: at the center of attention. Not for much longer, though. The Gaian prince had yet to show his face at the ball, but the moment Francisco Batista de la Reina did, all eyes would swing to him.

Like so many other elements of the Kingdom, the palace's ballroom had been modeled on the height of classical European style, though at a scale that the architects of that era could never have imagined. Four stories high, no less than six glittering crystal chandeliers, each the size of a minibus, hung on golden chains from a ceiling covered in rich murals. Ivory-colored columns framed the walls, each topped by the gold-leafed bust of the human form in divine perfection. Under their feet: floors made with slabs of golden tile, interrupted at regular intervals with exquisite mosaics. The only thing that outshone such fetching design was the compliment of its company: titans of industry, masters of the arts, creators of culture (for whom the exuberant access fees were paid by "patrons," but whom most people called "sugars"), and the dirty, filthy, stinking rich. By requirement, the costumes matched the motif: ballgowns and fine suits cost a pretty penny to code, and it showed.

When the invitations had first gone out to the highest tier of kingdom society, many weren't sure what to make of it. Gaia generally kept to itself, and that's the way they preferred it. A prince had never revealed himself to the public prior to the end of his five-year term of office, his identity concealed to avoid approach by interested parties. The de facto world government created a convenient mask, and its actions and wars, a distraction on the wires each evening. Meanwhile, the true global power brokers came to the Kingdom, a dalliance of a platform that provided the backdrop for all they wanted to be done.

Francisco Batista hadn't revealed himself publicly, per se, but the fact that he'd created this event in order to, as the invitation had said, "make acquaintance with the patrons of our sister city," had everyone on edge. Everyone, that was, except Kaylie. As the daughter of Johanna Tieg, and a high-level manager at Plaxis, she scoffed at the idea that Gaia could interfere with this land in which *she* ruled, socially if not actually.

And, if she played her cards right, even that would change.

"Good evening, pet."

Frederick Helsing slid her direction, his fine hips carrying a muscular frame she'd had the pleasure of inspecting at length only a week before. Dressed in a modern interpretation of baroque couture befitting the platform, he still managed to stand apart from the crowd with his good looks alone. She wasn't certain how much of his avatar was based on his real-world self; she'd been too scared of disappointment to make an occasion to see him there, despite several overtures. Not to mention, he lived in Italy, or what remained of it, and Sienna simply was not in fashion these days.

"What a lovely gown." He placed a kiss across her knuckles. "I look forward to taking you out of it later."

She retracted her hand the moment he removed his lips. "Sorry, but I'm working tonight."

"Oh, dear." He feigned hurt, pushing a hand to his heart. "Does Mommy have you seducing senators again? Or perhaps a certain visiting dignitary?"

Johanna chose just that moment to arrive, her blonde hair pulled and pushed in such a twist of loops and weaves, it looked like an angry ocean.

"Mr. Helsing?" She laced her arm through Kaylie's, pulling the latter insistently to her side. "Would you mind if I borrowed Kaylie for a moment?"

Kaylie attempted an apology through a half-hearted grimace. She wasn't at all upset to be parted from so recent a beau. It was like eating at a fine restaurant; the experience and tastes were delightful, but one needed a sufficient space of time before another visit would be as appealing.

When they were far enough from the others, Johanna rounded.

"You are not here to randomly socialize."

"I know."

"And you are certainly not here to have one of your fairytale fucks."

Kaylie bit the inside of her mouth so hard that she'd have tasted blood in the real. "I know. I'm here to seduce royalty."

Johanna held the fury of a fire in her eyes. "I don't think you'll need to sleep with him, but I'll leave that to your judgement. What I do need you to do is to be on Francisco like chips on silicon from the moment he arrives. Make sure he doesn't hobnob with anyone who would cause trouble for us later. And for god's sake, keep him from the Coeur. He might be intending to explore."

"You mean like he was exploring Plaxis two weeks ago?" the blonde snapped at her mother. "I still can't believe you even let him in the door, almost as much as I can't believe that you waited until yesterday to tell me who he really was."

Johanna sneered. "The terms of a Non-Disclosure Agreement have always baffled you, haven't they?"

Before her daughter could protest, Johanna immediately jumped back in. "As for letting him in: I didn't have a choice. Plaxis's agreements with the Gaia Congress allow the elected monarch unfettered access to our facilities. To have denied him would have caused more problems than it solved." Johanna turned her eyes across the dance floor filled with swishing dresses and clicking heels, up past the grand staircase, to where a second, hidden staircase lay behind a secret door. "I can't risk anyone finding out about Rex."

Kaylie forced away the dissent she'd shown just moments before. "There's no change, then?"

Johanna shook her head. "And people are beginning to notice. Even Cindira is getting suspicious. If she finds out..."

"She won't." Her own troubles aside, Kaylie actually took a moment to think about the situation from her mother's perspective. What would she herself like to hear if the woman she loved were discovered in such a condition? "He can't stay like that forever, Mother. Pretty soon you'll need to..."

"If getting at the source code was as easy as wishing it, we'd have sated the prince the first time and not had to go through this ridiculous pantomime," Johanna snapped. She brought her gaze back to her daughter. "Mind Francisco. Let's get through this charade without any surprises, okay?"

And in a swirl of purple silk, Johanna was gone, mixing back among the guests.

TWENTY-THREE

CINDIRA FOLLOWED LAPORTE, despite the quick clip and regardless of how the unyielding material of her skirt made each step labored.

"I've never heard of the Coeur or Yuchi," she said as they came to a grand marble staircase and began to climb, her guide leading the way. "I thought I knew a lot about the Kingdom. Are there any other secrets I'm unaware of?"

"To know the answer to that question, miss, I'd have to know what you know. Sadly, that is impossible."

She didn't think Laporte chose his words without purpose. "Sadly?"

"As I mentioned, I am not aware of the details of your mother's death. It happened during one of the few processes during which I'm unaware of what's going on in the real."

"But even as we're here now, you're also still back at Plaxis in the vreal, guarding my body." Though what a mouse could do to help if someone discovered her was questionable. "What were you doing that was so consuming?"

Why did you leave my mother alone when she needed you most?

"Something your mother asked me to do." Laporte kept up the swift pace without any of the effort she herself felt. "I have a feeling that, if I were able to access your memories the way I can do with an artificial system, I might be able to find clues. Ones you may even be aware of but are unable to contextualize with your inferior human cognitive abilities."

The staircase narrowed as they reached the second floor and turned to ascend to the third. "Gee, Laporte, tell me what you really think."

"I don't say this to insult you, but it will not help our endeavors if you fail to remember my abilities and use them to your full advantage. I—"

Cindira harrumphed as she came crashing into Laporte's back.

Confused, she lifted her head to see what had frozen her companion's movements.

The woman before them had black eyes. Not just pupils, but the entire orb. Like an animal's, and yet, far deeper than any other creature she had ever seen. She didn't conform to the Kingdom's Eurocentric, seventeenth century norms, dressed instead in the garb of ancient Japan, right down to a katana sword which she bore before her. The implied threat didn't go over Cindira's head: namely, if she advanced, that sword would go *through* Cindira's head.

Laporte regained his footing even as he took Cindira's hand and pulled her to the same step on which he stood. "Yuchi, how are you?"

"That's Yuchi?" She found herself whispering, then immediately wondered at the effort. "You said it was a guy."

"A bot doesn't have a consistent gender, but your language defaults to male pronouns. He, she... Like me, Yuchi can be either."

"Or neither." The accent vaguely matched the persona, making her somehow even more awe-inspiring. Yuchi kept her eyes trained on Laporte. "Third floor access is restricted to Tier Zero users. *You* know this."

Cindira huffed. "There is no such thing as Tier Zero users."

Only to be refuted by Laporte moments later. "She is a Tier Zero user. Check her credentials."

Anxiety twisted her insides. Wasn't avoiding detection by Yuchi one of the things they had said they wanted to accomplish?

Yuchi's eyes became distant for a moment, the inky black stained by dots of colors, all popping in and out of view with great rapidity.

"She *is* a Tier Zero user." Yuchi turned to Cindira, sheathing her sword. The bot bent at the waist. "You may pass, Miss Grover."

Cindira rushed past the samurai, even as she corrected by instinct, "It's Tieg, actually."

She'd changed it after she'd moved in with her father. Her mother's legacy gave a teenage girl working her way through academic circles too much baggage to tow.

"Negative." Yuchi twisted at the hip, even while keeping her feet planted. "User's name is Omala Grover. Please provide your verification credentials to confirm."

It didn't take words for Cindira to know she'd messed up. Laporte wore the evidence in his expression. Suddenly, a woman who didn't care too much for how the world observed her, wanted nothing more than a mirror to confirm her suspicions.

Hands pressed to her face brought understanding. "This is my mother's avatar."

Yuchi's sword flew into a defensive position. "It is a breach of the user agreement to inhabit any avatar not registered to and linked with the user's account. You have openly admitted to this violation. As prescribed in the user agreement, your avatar will be immediately destroyed. Remain still as I—"

Laporte sprung, caging Yuchi in his grasp. The pair fell backward, each tumble and tuck on the stairs announced with a *clunk*.

Somehow, her guide still managed to speak through it like nothing abnormal was happening. "Third door on the right. Hurry, I'll deal with this."

At the second-floor landing, Laporte managed to knock the sword from Yuchi's hand.

"But—"

"Don't worry about me. I'm immortal here. You are not. Not yet. Now, go."

Not *yet*?

But there was no time to ask. Cindira raced forward, hoping that if it was true Laporte could take on any form he wanted, he really should transition to one with bigger muscles.

TWENTY-FOUR

CINDIRA PULLED BACK the sheer curtain, revealing a stained-glass window lit from behind, the image, a knight slaying a six-legged dragon. Only, instead of white-glazed panels to comprise the knight's face, was a void, a peephole where one could look out, the design hiding her features in plain sight.

Below, the typical scene of so many of the archaic animated films played out in faux flesh, bone, and blood. Gowns, suits, musicians donning powdered wigs and playing wooden instruments, chandeliers blazing with a hundred candles each, couples working their way through carefully rehearsed steps, servants (mostly male, and wearing dressed down styles of the wealthy and affluent users around them) with trays filled with the very food she'd seen being prepped not an hour before navigating the guests, a fountain shooting a chocolate stream into which several women were dipping bits of cake or fruit...

The fairy tale, just as marketed.

A glitch at the corner of her eye preceded Laporte's reappearance, as though he were some sort of wizard popping into existence at will.

"Laporte! You scared me." Cindira leapt back, her hand flattening on her chest. "Yuchi?"

"Is rebooting. The process, combined with some road blocks I was able to throw up, will take about an hour."

It wasn't much time, but it would have to be enough. She turned back to the window, studying the crowd below, looking for Francisco's face, though she found it increasingly difficult to focus. So many luxuries and baubles on which the eye could catch. Curiosity burned within her: who were these people, and why were they here?

Despite the situation, Cindira was enraptured. Awe was an understatement. She had coded individual artifacts, like Kaylie's intricate dresses, but the rich tapestry of the full view before her...how was it possible this was not *real*?

"You are impressed." It was a statement, not a question.

Cindira couldn't bring herself to lie, despite a little voice inside her reminding her that her mother never wanted this. "How could I not be? Gaia is amazing, but its buildings, its landscapes... Even the virtual weapons armies use to face each other in the Arenas of War... They're all direct reproductions of things that exist in the real. But these things...the fashion, the style, the building...this hasn't existed for hundreds of years, but there it all *is*."

"Despite the old saying, miss, I don't believe you only get one chance to make a *first* impression." Laporte pointed to the crowd below. "From up here, you see the big picture, the illusion of the cover story. Look *closer*. Look into the subtext of what really lies before you."

She need only to relax her gaze to see through the noise and take in the nuance as Laporte narrated the scene.

"That couple dancing there?" he said, pointing. "The prime minister and president of two countries currently warring inside Gaia, laughing and smiling as though they hadn't a care in the world. The lanky man standing at the fountain who'd just popped a strawberry in his mouth? A prime minister elected with questionable legitimacy, who just a few weeks ago had been indicted by the Gaian court of real world war crimes."

Laporte pivoted, this time indicating the far end of the ballroom where a woman who'd retreated to a mezzanine invisible to those below remained in plain sight of their current position. She grinned as a man accompanying her and dressed to the nines pushed her to the ground, lifted her skirt, and shoved his head into the folds of muslin, disappearing from view.

"Mira Labati, the famous actress currently on trial for killing her husband, and the journalist whose been assigned by *Tiempo Nuevo* to cover the case. He's not a member, of course. She provided him a guest pass for the evening, and I don't think she intended it just for the Kingdom but for her bedchamber."

The sparkling garden she'd taken for the Kingdom just moments before began to show its rot. Cindira's face screwed up as the shifting expression Labati wore suggested she was having a much better time than most.

"In public? She just has him go down on her... in the open? And no one says anything?"

"To raise your mouth here is to raise your hand, volunteering to have your dirt exposed as you threaten to expose others. That, combined with the pain safeties being disabled..."

"They're turned off?"

Cindira couldn't imagine the consequence. One of the reasons the vreal was so engaging was because of one's ability to take risks without worry. It might cause a moment of panic if you were to, say, fall off a tall building, but in the real, you'd be fine. Unless the safeties were turned off, that was, in which case the interface would transfer the *experience* of the pain into the real.

"Do our engineers know? Are they working on a solution?" She was certain she could code one in no time at all if they weren't sure how.

"Miss, I'm afraid you don't understand. The safeties are disabled *intentionally*." With eyes much sadder than any non-human's should be, Laporte gazed at Cindira. "Plaxis promises the chance to relive a romantic past, but the past was never romantic. This world never existed. It still doesn't." Her companion shook his head. "Your mother dreamed of a world united, where disputes and conflict could be resolved in the interest of peace and prosperity, without destroying lands or lives. And then, Plaxis held up a mirror to her vision, everything reflecting here, backward. Everything that Gaia is, this is the opposite. If your mother had lived, she would have done everything in her power to keep this from prospering. And your father..."

Suddenly, Cindira's heart raced. "What about him?"

His eyes dropped to the floor. "When you said you intended to come here, I thought I should stop you. You've placed yourself in tremendous harm just by jacking in. But I also knew it was an opportunity for you to learn the truth."

"Laporte." Cindira turned from the window, forgetting the swirling plays of indulgence below. "My father is on an extended business trip. Why are you bringing him up now?"

The mouse-turned-man stepped away from the window and towards a wardrobe that sat on the edge of the room, a monstrously huge thing styled to look of mahogany and cherry wood. Inside, there were no blankets or linens or even dresses. There was an archway, and beyond that, another room.

With a hand gestured toward what lay beyond her field of vision, Laporte invited her to see past the fairy tale and discover the facts. "I'm afraid he may be a victim of it."

"Dad!" Cindira rushed to the four-poster bed festooned with richly-embroidered green curtains. "Oh, my god, Dad. You're here! Where you have you been for so long? I was—"

Words cut off as confusion crept in. Everything about the Kingdom was impractical, but none of it until now had been impossible. What Cindira saw defied her understanding of the vreal. The avatar was definitely her father's, but he was either pretending to be asleep, or something had terribly, terribly malfunctioned.

"What's wrong with him?" She leaned over the bed, giving her dad's shoulders a gentle shake. "Why isn't he responding? "

The man beside her recalled his mouse behaviors when his head twitched, examining the sight before them. "The most recent entry recording your father's arrival to the palace grounds was two months ago, but I find no exit record for him after that time."

"Two *months*?" Rage turned to worry. Cindira sat on his bed, stroking her father's stubble-strewn cheek. "You mean that my father's been lying here like this the whole time he's been supposed in China?"

"I cannot say. As you'll recall, I can only detect when someone passes a checkpoint into another section of the platform; I cannot tell where within that section they've been or are." Laporte circled the bed and sat on the opposite side. "I became aware of his presence and condition a few weeks ago. His avatar appears to be in stasis."

"Stasis? What, you mean like a coma?" A crushing weight materialized in her stomach. "Or are you saying my father is dead?"

Laporte shook his head. "I can't say for certain. This isn't like you and your mother's avatars. Omala made those to be permanently accessible, but not your father's. If jacked out, his avatar should have gone into the dormant files, as all others do. But I don't want you to think this means he's dead, miss. I have no evidence to suggest that conclusion."

"Do you have any evidence he's alive?"

Laporte's silence spoke louder than words.

The anxiety that had smoked her soul rose into the sky and dissipated. The bounce faded when her analytical mind raced to piece together what had happened. Two months was a long time to be missing without anyone noticing, but Cindira had noticed. When she went to Johanna, her stepmother always had an excuse. *"He's still in Asia." "There was need for him to stop in Istanbul." "An urgent request from one of our partners in Bangalore."* It seemed unlikely that Johanna would have been unaware of the truth, that Rex Tieg was black boxed inside the Kingdom.

The glitch was exceedingly rare, but it happened once or twice a year. Something would go wrong with an entry or exit and the user's avatar and mind would end up somewhere in the abyss of code, unable to go one way or another. But that problem was one easily solved. Why hadn't Johanna solved it, then? PR? The implications of the CEO of the company being stuck?

Or was there a reason she didn't want this fixed?

"If he isn't dead, is it possible that he's in a..."

Then, suddenly, Laporte, as if by magic, ceased to exist.

A different voice filled the void. "Who are you?"

Cindira shot to her feet and even considered running, but it would do no good. Johanna was between her and the only door in or out of the room. Keeping her face to her father, her back to her stepmother, Cindira turned her head over her shoulder only enough to see the snake that had her cornered.

Johanna stepped with deliberate precision, the skirting of the very dress that Cindira herself had designed only the night before swaying like the head of a cobra. "You're not a servant VAPOR, even though you're dressed like one. Who are you and how did you get in here?"

Cindira kept her face turned away from her stepmother, the cloth around her head shielding her face. "I'm..." *His daughter.* But she wasn't. At least, not when she was using her mother's avatar.

"Someone concerned for his safety."

"You suppose I am not?" Venom laced Johanna's tone. "If you were so concerned for his safety, you wouldn't keep him like this. You'd free him."

What the hell? "You think *I* did this to him?"

"Do you suppose I did? Why would I put my own husband into a coma?"

"Because it gives you unchecked control of Plaxis." Cindira labored to keep her tone flat, the timbre of her mother's voice concealed. "I know who you are, Johanna Tieg. I know how you love power and influence and money—all of which you've been consolidating for years."

"All of which I've offered to you. But no, you only want what I can't supply."

Her father and stepmother were some of the most powerful and wealthy people in the western world, if not the planet. Who were the people holding her father, and what could they possibly want that Johanna couldn't provide them on demand?

What had Laporte been hiding from her?

Cindira's curiosity screeched to a halt as manicured fingernails bit into her shoulder. She cried out, even as Johanna spun her around. Cindira regained her footing only in time to look up and see her stepmother lose her own. The woman stumbled backward in shock.

"Impossible."

This programming? So robust. Johanna's skin blanched, her pupils dilated. Her stepmother threw a hand over her mouth, the diaphanous material of the dress sleeve Cindira herself had designed, billowed.

"Omala?"

TWENTY-FIVE

"THERE'S STILL TIME to change your mind."

Francisco pulled back as the door to the kitchens swung closed. That there was a kitchen in the Kingdom surprised him. That was a change. No one ever ate food while logged into Gaia. Coffee remained a mainstay, though only because the habit was so ingrained in the real world, those transitioning to the virtual one for work found it difficult to go without. Even rendered as an avatar, psychological dependencies proved tough to defeat.

But as the prince came to terms with that fact, he remembered it was only one small part of the larger picture in this platform, one tailored for indulgences without consequence. Of course, there was food. More food in this one palace than in all the peasant kitchens of his homeland combined, likely. And as he looked out on the dance floor, he saw it was merely one excess this world boasted.

His trusted attaché, Carlos, waited as ever he did; tolerantly, silently, reverently. He had the patience of a saint and the combat skills of a warlord.

Francisco shook his head. "No. When I campaigned for office last year, I vowed to the Congress that ferreting out the corruption that goes on here would be my top priority."

"No one takes a campaign promise at face value, Your Highness."

"I do." He turned back, pushing the swinging door just enough to give himself a view of the ballroom beyond. "Gaia saved the world from destruction, Carlos, but that hit the bank accounts of many people in that room out there – at least one of whom is trying to destroy Gaia now. Most likely, more than one. They want me to cower, to stay hidden. I'm here to show them I'm not afraid."

"One might suggest you *should* be," Carlos cautioned. "They've penetrated Gaia's security, a system that has remained unhackable for a quarter century, not once but three times in as many weeks. There is no reason to think they'd be any less lethal in the real. Pretending to be one of them may backfire in more ways than you've imagined."

"You forget, I was one of them. Maybe I am still, the way I exploited my position."

His thoughts turned back to his visit to Plaxis, and playing into Kaylie Fife's flirtations, just to get to the truth he was seeking. His stomach had turned with every touch. In a few minutes, he'd repeat the process, and this time, backing out after getting to the answer of a simple yes or no question wouldn't be possible. He needed to seduce her, get her to trust him. Either she knew the truth of what was going on inside of Gaia, or she knew the people who did. *She associates with all the power brokers. She's slept with many of them.* In the virtual world, at least, his spies had told him. His analyst argued on whether or not she was simply the kind of woman who liked to boast of rendezvous with the famous and powerful, or if plots lay underneath her conquests. Francisco suspected the latter; she was the daughter of Johanna Tieg. A snake gave birth to snakes, and once he came to know her better, he suspected he'd find a serpent in his grasp.

A mirror mounted over a nearby sink let him check his hair with an informed eye. Later, he'd wonder at the washbasin's presence. Did this vreal world really have need of disinfectant? For now, he needed to be prepared. In a moment, he'd be walking openly among the enemy.

"I don't expect to find out who's behind the attacks on the capital tonight. If I make them believe I'm still one of them, I think it could lead to the anarchists outing themselves. *The secret lies in confusing the enemy, so that he cannot fathom your true intentions.*"

"Sun Tzu." Carlos allowed him an approving nod. "An appropriate tome to study for the times. But I believe he also said, *The wise warrior avoids battle.*"

"Yes, but wasn't it rumored that he, himself, died in battle?"

Francisco's attaché raised a scrupulous eyebrow. "If *he* ever truly existed at all."

"If any of us do." Enough. No more stalling. "Wish me luck, Carlos."

"Luck is for those who have no faith in liberty."

Francisco pushed the door open and observed in amazement as

a room full of theatrics turned its spotlight on him. In the span of a moment, his courage fled back in time, and he saw himself as a youth, trembling on the stairs of his family's veranda, watching his father's blood trickle down each step. The people turned to him expectant, some perhaps ignoble. He could see it in their eyes: *So, this is the great prince without a kingdom who thinks he can challenge us?*

He wondered the same thing. His father's watch felt tighter on his wrist suddenly.

Francisco opened his mouth to speak, for they seemed to want him to say something. But what could he say? *I know one of you has been trying to kill me? I suspect one of you is trying to destroy Gaia?* It wasn't exactly diplomatic.

As he felt an arm weave through his and turned to see who was at his side, he thanked God for small miracles. Until, that was, he realized the woman suddenly plastered at his side was none other than Kaylie Fife.

"Your Majesty?" Her wet eyes shone as if animated. "I was beginning to worry you were going to skip out on the party, which would make you an intolerably bad host. Having cold feet about joining the soiree?"

Francisco knew how to play the game. Putting on his best public face, he grinned as though the woman beside him had just said the most amazing thing. "Of course not, Miss Fife. I've been anticipating it all week." With a small wave, he acknowledged the crowd without looking at anyone in particular. *That's* what royalty did, after all. It was rude to ignore. It was belittling to distinguish.

Kaylie leaned in, talking so only he could hear, even as the other guests began to shuffle. Toward him to ingratiate, away from him to remain aloof. "Just stay by my side. I'll make sure you only have to talk to the right people."

He bit his tongue, fighting back the truth he already knew.

There were no right people in this place.

And that included him.

TWENTY-SIX

CINDIRA'S FUTURE BALANCED on a single decision: let Johanna believe her rival was indeed facing her down, admit to being Cindira, or keep both facts hidden.

She pulled herself erect, trying to embody her mother's mannerisms. "I'm not who you think I am."

Johanna threw back her head and cackled, balled-up fists planted on her hips. "I know exactly who you are. You're the Bandit."

Bandit? What was she talking about? Part of Cindira wanted to slide along that tangent and see where it took her. She couldn't, though. She was running out of time; Yuchi would be back online soon enough, and when she was, Cindira would be toast. Before she could pan out the pros and cons of assuming control, she was simply doing it.

Cindira pointed at the bed. "This avatar belongs to Rex Tieg. Why is he like this? What are his current whereabouts in the real?"

"It's me who should ask you that. Instead, let me ask how you designed an avatar that looks and sounds exactly like Omala Grover?" The blonde bit her lip in momentarily contemplation. "There was one still hidden somewhere, wasn't there? I've heard rumors for years, that she had cubby holes all over the platform that no one could find except her. I guess it was only a matter of time before someone like you stumbled across one."

Cindira wouldn't be detoured. "What are you doing to try and resolve this?"

Johanna's head tilted to the side. "Exactly what you told me: I lured the prince here, even made him think it was his idea. He suspects nothing. If there's anything he knows about the source code, Kaylie will get it out of him."

"If *he* knows anything about it?" Confused, Cindira blinked several times in succession. "But he came to Plaxis asking *you* about it."

"He was feeling out abilities, obviously. I'm not sure what his agenda is, but Francisco isn't like his predecessors. He seems to actually believe he can do some good with his power instead of thinking his power could do him some good." Johanna folded her arms over her chest. "I guess I shouldn't be surprised you knew about his visit. I always suspected you had a spy in the Kitchens."

She bit down in frustration. Cindira could have kicked herself. How could she forget so few people knew what Batista looked like in the real? Not that that was going to be true after tonight. He was parading around downstairs in an avatar designed as his real doppelganger. She could figure out if it was because he was so brave, or because he was so arrogant.

The code writer was equally skilled in math and added up the figures pretty quickly. "You told Kaylie to seduce him."

"I told her to distract him," Johanna said. "That is what you wanted, isn't it? Besides, if the prince finds out that our CEO is being held for ransom, do you think he'll stay jacked in here? If the public knows, what do you think will happen to Plaxis? Your ends, as hideous as they are, require my company to stay robust."

"A human life isn't worth the cash flow of your hedonistic escape." Cindira balled her hands into fists as she took one more look at her father on the bed. "You've made a mockery of Omala Grover's legacy, and there will be consequences. He should not be one."

"There now, you've found your standard script again." Her stepmother sat herself on the edge of the bed, stroking Rex's face. "I don't know how much you knew about Omala—the *real* Omala—but she wasn't exactly Rex's fan at the end, and she wasn't the squeaky-clean 'goddess' those crazy chipheads hold her out to be. In fact, she was actively trying to destroy Plaxis. Of course, that's what you and your cult want too, isn't it?"

Something about the way Johanna broke down before her, how her complete focus was on the man in the bed as she raised his hand to her mouth, kissed his palm, and then pressed it against her cheek, cracked Cindira's resolve. *Johanna may be a power-hungry, fame-seeking, money-grubbing nuisance, but the woman does love her husband.* And Rex? Despite the fact that he'd left Cindira's mother, turning his back on his child and the legacy they'd built together, one couldn't claim with any validity that he didn't feel the same for Johanna.

Cindira backed away from the bed. "Will you continue to protect his avatar here?"

"Why else would I do everything you ask of me? I can't lose him."

Temptation called on Cindira to try and convince Johanna that she wasn't this *Bandit* person. The only way to do that, however, was to suggest who she really might be. Wasn't there something she could say, some sort of comfort she could give? She didn't like Johanna, but that didn't mean she wanted her to suffer needlessly. And if Cindira was going to find out what was really happening with her father, she would need her stepmother's cooperation.

Once I figure out how to even bring up the subject with her in the real.

"You will see him again, just... do what you're told." *Don't give them a reason to hurt Dad.*

Johanna lifted wet eyes. "I will do whatever it takes, but as I've told you before: if you hurt Rex, of if you come after one of my children, then one day when I find out who you are, I *will* kill you." She swallowed a lump in her throat. "Just like I killed the woman whose avatar you wear."

"Just like you—"Cindira froze.

It wasn't possible.

"You *killed* Omala Grover?"

No, it couldn't be.

"You..." Her hands folded over her heart. "Everyone thinks she was knocked unconscious by that boat and drowned."

"She did. *Technically*. But I was the one who pushed her into the water at just the right moment, and that *beautiful sari* she wore that night probably made treading water just about impossible."

Suddenly, Johanna leaned into the bed, her hand snaking under Rex's pillow. Then, without warning, she leapt up. In her hand she clutched a silver blade, and in her eyes, fury burned red.

"I'm going to try a much more direct method with you though." Johanna paced forward, Cindira retreating in equal measure. "It was stupid of you to come here. Didn't you know that if you die in the Kingdom, you die in the real? It's a nice little safety measure we have to keep everyone... *honest.*"

Cindira's arm presented a weak shield before her. "But if you kill me, you'll never find out what happened to Rex."

"But I'm willing to bet someone will find your body. And when they do, I'll know who you are, and I'll run down every account you hold, friend you've had, or book you read until I find him. Say good-bye, Bandit."

Johanna lunged. Cindira fell back. Her arm went up and she prepared herself for pain. But nothing came.

And then...

A wall of white shot up between her and Johanna, a wall of flame both impenetrable and transparent. Johanna's volley flattened, spread out as if it had been hurled into a shield.

A myriad of different voices spoke in unison. "Run Cindira, or you'll never save your father!"

Cindira didn't know whose voice it was, or where it came from, but it snapped her out of her spell. She bolted towards the door. She had to get out of there.

She had to get free and find her father.

TWENTY-SEVEN

"AND THIS..." KAYLIE pulled on Francisco's arm, leading him to yet another elegantly-dressed couple, "Is Nugato Shoji and his wife, Kiki."

Instead of offering a hand, the gentleman bowed, a gesture somewhat archaic but still practiced in some areas of Asia. Francisco returned the gesture.

"Sir. Madame."

"Miss Fife." Another of the attendees begged Kaylie's attention. They all turned to see a servant VAPOR, the diamond-shaped mark between his eyes radiating a dull blue. "Your attention is required momentarily in the kitchen."

His young, attractive hostess sneered to the bot before turning back to her guests. "Would you excuse me a moment? Your Majesty—" She gave Francisco a saccharine grin. "—I'll be right back. Don't wander away."

If up to him, Francisco would run full speed from the castle. It was the first moment since he'd arrived that his left arm had been free of Kaylie's pull. But what would be the point of having come here at all if he did? Attending this ball had been his idea, a chance to meet the powerbrokers of the real in their elite, exclusive little club. So far, the only people he had met were ones Kaylie had curated for him: lower level but wealthy merchants, a few celebrities, a pair of Cardinals. She was keeping him caged with that arm, and as soon as he could break free of these two without being rude, he might finally sink his teeth into the intrigues swirling around him.

"So this is the brave Prince of Gaia." Kiki passed judgement with both tone and a shaded eye. "They say your avatar is true to your real-world self. How disappointing."

"I think what Kiki is trying to say—" Nugato side-eyed his wife, who only rolled hers in turn. "—is that we're surprised you're brave enough to show your true face. So few in the Kingdom do."

"Something I believe should change," the prince said. "How can we negotiate terms of peace and trade in good faith if we cannot even take each other at face value? Though, I admit, I think minor cosmetic edits are okay." He pointed to his left ear. "There's actually a scar here in real life."

The slightest scent of possible scandal filled the air, and the shark bit. Kiki's tone pitched up, the speed with which she spoke more jovial.

"A scar?" She leaned in closer, as though she could see it if she only squinted hard enough. "How exciting. From what?"

"When I was fourteen, mercenaries broke into my family's home and killed my father in front of my eyes. One smashed the heel of his blaster over my head to knock me out. I woke up with my father's corpse staring at me from the stairs. This scar is the only thing the revolutionaries left me with."

Francisco sipped his wine, even as Kiki scrambled for something to say.

She was saved by her husband weaving his arm through hers and saying, "Our sympathies for your loss," before leading her away.

Finally.

Francisco downed the rest of his drink without tasting anything. The wine wasn't the point. An empty glass gave him an excuse to move across the room to where a VAPOR stood behind a table laden with a dozen varieties of refreshment. The prince walked at a measured pace, picking up threads of conversation with each step. Those around the fringes didn't hesitate to engage in their standard business. An illegal trade deal was the least of the sins his ears tripped over. To his right, two men discussed the details of deep earth mineral extraction, a process that would ravage the lands above it. Gaia had outlawed the practice in the second year of its existence.

"A glass of red." Francisco handed his glass to the VAPOR, even as he saw another man pull up to the table beside him do the same.

A man who he hadn't seen in twenty years, and whom he had prayed never to see for as long as he lived.

"For me as well, thank you."

It couldn't be. Eyes slammed shut, Francisco's heart exploded, his pulse pushing away awareness. Could someone have an anxiety attack in the vreal? Would the pain suppressors dull the ache? Francisco realized they weren't. His chest ached, even as the man beside him put a hand on his shoulder.

"Well, well, if it isn't His Majesty, *Prince* Francisco Batista de le Reina."

Francisco plastered on a plastic smile, forced his eyes open and schooled his expression into a professional passiveness.

Of all the people in the world to cross paths with in the vreal...

In a total reversal, Francisco prayed Kaylie would find him and recapture him. Surely she didn't want there to be a scene, and how could there not be when Francisco was suddenly forced to face the man he'd once called friend.

"Not going to say anything?" Hugo smirked.

The prince rounded, his eyes scanning the crowd for his heretofore undesired escort. With no choice but to confront his past head on, he found his spine and put it to good use.

Francisco pushed a hand forward. The confidence might be conjured, but diplomacy called for a skill. "Hugo Ferrente de Miguel."

He'd expected to see the wizened, battle-scarred face of his lifelong adversary, framed in graying, spiked hair and with one eye bandaged over, lost in one of the last real-world skirmishes to take place on the Iberian Peninsula before the region dedicated itself to the Gaia platform. Instead, a younger iteration of his former friend, skin as perfect and unblemished as it had been when they were youths, greeted him.

Hugo's smile fell as his grip on Francisco's hand tightened. "You forgot to say *Duque*."

"It's one of my life's ambitions to do so." Francisco pulled the glass to his lips, talking over the rim. "Something wrong with your own platform? Or are you here spying on the competition?"

"It's not spying as much as it is market research. Don't worry; the Tiegs know I'm a client. They had to approve my membership personally. I don't think they're particularly threatened by me. Tagentry would never offer something quite this lux. It's not really our vibe."

Hugo paused to accept his glass back from the VAPOR. "So, Prince of Gaia? I have to admit, I was surprised to learn you'd put yourself up for election. I was astonished even more when you won."

"Yes, well, Gaia was founded primarily for the benefit of the poor and powerless, both of which your family's overthrow of my family left me. So really, I've just become a leader to my own people."

"Oh, come now, Francisco. You've done okay for yourself. And don't tell me there aren't certain—" Hugo looked up and caught Kaylie's eye as she started to work her way across the room. "—*benefits* to being in your position."

Francisco followed Hugo's gaze. "As well as some detriments."

"Really, so you and Kaylie aren't..." His voice tapered off.

The prince took another sip of his wine, wishing the effects of it in the vreal were more tangible. "I would never stoop so low."

"That's a terrible thing to say about one of the most desired women in the realm."

"If you want a shot of her, Hugo, by all means."

Hugo grinned but said nothing. Francisco must have called his bluff without even realizing it. Well, at least his former friend had some standards.

Though it would be so much easier to hate him if he didn't respect that decision.

"I heard you ran on a platform of stomping out corruption. Is that why you're here? To find someone to make an example of?"

"I'm here to show my face. I'm here to let everyone know that I'm not like the last prince, or the princess before, that I'm not going to cower from threats. I'm not interested in being the custodian of the wardomes. I'm in the office to make sure that what happens in them has meaning in the real once everyone jacks out."

"A noble endeavor." Hugo bobbed his head. "But I wonder, how much do you think you'll accomplish when someone finds out about *your* past?"

"You mean the part where your uncle's hired goons shot my father and grandfather in the head right in front of me?"

Hugo huffed a laugh under his breath. "No, I mean the part where you tried to destroy all this, and almost got away with it too."

Ice ran through Francisco's veins. Every muscle in his body tensed. "How could you possibly—"

"I know, the court records were sealed because you were a minor," Hugo said, cutting him off. "The thing about seals is, they have a way of loosening with time." Pulling back, Hugo offered his hand again. "It was good to catch up, Francisco."

But the prince ignored him. A moment later, Hugo gave one more knowing cocky grin, and then, was gone.

"There you are." Kaylie finally managed to catch up with them. She leaned over the table, catching a glass the VAPOR had just filled for someone else. "Was that Hugo Ferrente you were talking with? That man is a bastard."

For once, Francisco found himself agreeing with his hostess. "Yes. Yes, he is."

TWENTY-EIGHT

CINDIRA TURNED A CORNER and found another hall. There was no end of doors in this place. Where could they all go? She ran to the first. Locked. The second, then the third. No luck. The fourth mercifully opened to a set of service stairs. Here, no unnatural luminescence lit her path. Instead, candles flickered on sconces that lined the walls. Her feet ate up the distance, each step pronounced by the *click, clank, click* of her glass shoes. Finally, she came to a landing, another hall, and a single door.

Please, please, please, let it be unlocked. A quick look over her shoulder informed her that Johanna still hadn't caught up with her, but she had no doubt she would. Her stepmother must know these halls and how best to navigate them. Cindira was pushing forward and making way by dumb luck. In her mind, she strung together code, a simple decryption matrix, and visualized it against the structure before her. The lock unclicked just as her hand settled on the knob and turned.

And suddenly, there he was.

"The prince."

She'd ended up in the ballroom with no idea how she'd gotten there. Did it matter? *He* was the reason she snuck into the Kingdom to begin with, and with the crowd around, Johanna would have a harder time finding her. *Frank* stood on the other side of the room, anchored in place by Kaylie's arm, as they chatted with a small group of people. It was funny. When he'd come to Plaxis, he'd impressed her by not being that impressive. She still remembered his monochromatic way of dressing, like he was trying to blend in with the background. What a transformation he'd made. His suit was still only black and white, but the cut was appropriate for the aesthetic. His black baroque-era jacket had such delicate white embroidery along its edges and up the collar that it must have taken the coders a week to make the design. His short pants cut off at the knees, where black stockings covered his calves and ankles, a pair of leather boots on his feet. An ivory vest peaked out from under the jacket, and a bunch of lace at his throat drew attention to his prominent chin and supple lips, framed by the hint of facial hair.

He was exactly the man he'd been when she'd first seen him, and yet, something more in a way she couldn't quite define. She realized then that it wasn't the way he looked, it was how he acted. Here, he was in his element. It was the Kingdom after all, and Francisco was holding court.

"Go to him!"

Cindira squealed as something small and furry crawled over her foot. "Laporte?"

He was a mouse again, which was just as well. He certainly was more portable that way, and if there was one thing she needed, it was to keep moving.

"Sorry I disappeared," he said as she picked him up. "Johanna doesn't know about me, and it's best if that remains the case."

Even though he wasn't real, even though he was just the manifestation of codes, algorithms, and AI, he was the closest thing to a confidante she had. Maybe that was why she found herself confessing to him. "She killed my mother."

The mouse blinked. "What?"

"Johanna killed my mother," Cindira said. "She just told me. She just... Oh, my god. All this time, for years, and I...my father is..."

"Miss, I hate to sound uncaring. We *will* use this knowledge, but for now, you are here. If you're to speak with the prince, it must be now," Laporte, balancing on her shoulder, advised. "Time is running out. We have twenty minutes until Yuchi recovers, and we must get you out before then."

Why was that important? "Didn't you hear what I said? My mother is dead, and Johanna killed her."

"And will you just sit here and allow her to do the same to you?"

"Of course not. But how could she? You can't die in the—"

Laporte cut her off. "The Kingdom isn't like Gaia. Here, if you die in the program, you die in the real."

Her blood became ice. "But that's against every international law written. It's murder!"

"It's the least of Plaxis's offenses."

She shook her head, trying to fit in this revelation with the company run by her father. "How often does that—"

"I can tell you the details later. For now, focus. Find the prince. Do what you came here to do. You're unlikely to have another chance like this."

But the wheels in Cindira's mind refused to halt. The implications of such a policy sprinted down a tree of logic, leading to one, single inevitable conclusion.

So that was why Johanna had agreed to let Francisco host this ball.

Cindira was up and moving into the ballroom before Laporte could even complete the sentence. "Someone's going to kill him."

TWENTY-NINE

CINDIRA OBSERVED HOW the VAPORs carried themselves, attempting to reproduce their algorithmic step-and-sway at the same time. A throng of clients swirling or milling in their exquisite period attire paid her no mind, despite how she must have looked like she was malfunctioning. Dressing in servant clothes rendered her functionally invisible. Even if she was wearing her mother's avatar, it might not be noticeable thanks to the frock covering her hair and the blue bhindi between her eyes. Laporte really knew what he was doing by disguising her.

Kaylie had become a barnacle on the side of the ship of state. She and the prince weren't that far away. Ten, fifteen feet? Cindira could probably shout Francisco's name and he'd hear. The trick lay in finding a way to talk with him without Kaylie noticing. If only there was some way that she could be invisible to everyone in the room except for the prince, this would all be so much easier.

"I have to get him out of here."

Under the cover of her head frock, the mouse sniffed. "Why? I thought you only wanted to talk to him."

"That was before I realized the danger he's in." Cindira looked around, thankful that the clients were still blind to her absence, especially given that they might think she was muttering to herself. "The explosion in Gaia would have killed us both if it didn't have the safety protocols in it. If someone tries that here, he won't survive. And why wouldn't they try?"

Cindira looked back over her shoulder just in time to see a swish of purple petticoats push through the door that she'd come through moments before. The knife had been stowed away, but she didn't think for a moment that Johanna wasn't still armed.

"Laporte, how much time is there between Yuchi coming back online and the stroke of midnight protocol activates?"

"Ten minutes, ten seconds."

Ten minutes of vulnerability? She'd have to make it work.

"Can you summon that coach to the front steps?"

The mouse chirped. "I'll have to drive it myself, but yes. I'll need two minutes, miss, then I'll be outside. Just there, at the far end of the room."

She turned, seeing a set of open double doors beyond which the light of the ballroom danced over cobblestones and a fountain. Even from the occluded rear view, Cindira recognized the ceremonial entrance at the front of the palace from Plaxis's marketing materials.

"Don't be late," she told the mouse.

Laporte scurried off her shoulder, down her skirting, and deftly wove between hundreds of feet to the front entrance. The clock was ticking. She couldn't waste time. Cindira needed to get to the prince and then get him out of the Kingdom before his would-be assassin had time to come up with a counteroffensive.

And that was assuming the prince didn't just dismiss her out of hand. Of course, he would, why hadn't she thought of that. If she only had time to plan! Cindira had the mind of a programmer: one piece of code led to the next led to the next. Take away a step, and the action couldn't execute. She knew she needed to get the prince to safety, but she couldn't think of the line that came before that to make it possible. With each step, her footfalls became harder.

But the moment Johanna rushed past her, her purple petticoats swishing from side to side, her footsteps ceased all together.

Heart pounding, Cindira buried her chin into her chest and turned, her back to the threesome that formed with her stepmother's arrival, and gingerly side-walked so she was right behind them, out of their direct line of sight.

"Mom, you look..." Kaylie's voice stretched. "Off."

"We have a hacker in our midst." Johanna labored to even her breaths. "Your Majesty, you should attempt a cool and quiet exit as soon as possible. You could be in danger."

For a moment, Cindira's tensions ebbed, until Kaylie spoke and ramped them right back up again.

"Don't be silly. There's less than ten minutes until midnight. He's safer here, surrounded by everyone, instead of rushing off alone.

The protocols will activate and force out the hacker, and the party can continue with no one the wiser."

Kaylie was right. But that wouldn't save Francisco from the real threat. As soon as Yuchi kicked Cindira out, whomever had designs on him could just accomplish their task even easier.

"Ms. Tieg, do you know who they are?" If the prince felt in any danger, evidence of it wasn't in his voice. His tone was as calm and as even as if he'd been asking about the weather. "Do you know what they want?"

"I don't know what she's after. I followed her down here from the Couer, but I don't see her anywhere. Look around. She can't be that hard to find. She's dressed like a servant VAPOR, but she has the face of... Of an old acquaintance of mine."

Cindira could practically feel their eyes rove the crowd. She was only a few feet away. Even with her back turned, it should be easy enough to see her. Why couldn't they?

"Not hard to find?" Kaylie's words dripped with sarcasm. "Mother, there have to be fifty servant VAPORS drifting around."

"If you used your authority to turn off the VAPORs, then the one's that left would be her."

Francisco's suggestion was both simple and terrifying. Cindira clutched at her throat.

"No," Johanna barked. "That might cause a panic among the crowd. Maybe the prince is right. Maybe we should just stay here and wait for Yuchi to solve the problem for us."

"And if this hacker of yours decides to tempt fate anyway?" Francisco asked.

The sound that Cindira heard put a chill in her blood, like a sword being drawn from a sheath or a blade worked over a whetting stone. Pulling down her head frock so it didn't bunch up, Cindira looked back over her shoulder and saw Johanna had indeed retained her weapon. The knife was hidden behind her back, but ready to strike should the need arise.

Johanna was putting a possible murder weapon within an arm's length of the prince, with an unknown threat somewhere in the room?

Cindira couldn't let her get away with it. She had the blade in hand and pressed to Francisco's throat before she could give the plan, or the idea that this was *real*, too much thought.

"Nobody move and I won't harm him." Luckily, he wasn't much taller than she was, or this impromptu act would have been over before it'd begun. It also kept her face blocked from the crowd. No telling what the consequences would be if Omala Grover was suddenly seen in the vreal, kidnapping the sovereign of Gaia.

The prince managed nonchalance and threw his hands up in the air. "I don't know who you are, but I will. Everyone will. Let me go now, and you stand a chance at surviving this."

The crowd hushed, pulling back in a rush as though they were the ones under threat. All except Kaylie, who planted her balled up fists on her hips (as well as could be done, given the corset she wore beneath her gown to hold it in the right shape), and took two steps forward, as if she was well and good going to do something about this. Only, before she could manage anything, Johanna pulled her behind her back. Maybe her stepmother did have some tenderness for her biological daughter.

The prince spoke softly, as though he didn't want the others to overhear. "What is it you're hoping to get away with? Slit my throat, it will—"

"Quiet!" She backstepped, leading them along the edge of the buffet table, towards the doors that led outside. There wasn't time to explain to him. If she didn't get him out of here and warn him of the true danger he was in before the midnight protocols swept her out, he'd really be in trouble. "Just... stay quiet and keep walking backwards."

He complied, all while chuckling lowly. "I never thought I'd be the kind of person to say this, but...do you know who I am?"

Francisco yelped as Cindira's arm jerked him back a little harder. "Do you think I'd be doing this if I didn't?"

"Then you must know there's no way you're going to get away with this."

"You should pray I do, or you're never going to survive tonight." Backing through the doors that lead to the gardens, she paused. "Close them."

He stayed frozen. "No."

Well, fine then.

Cindira paused and closed her eyes, concentrating to speed the process. She pictured the series of commands in her head, then pushed them out. When she opened her eyes, it was just in time to see the open doors swing close, then reconstituted themselves. Gone were the leaded frames, the panes of glass, the shiny metal knobs. Now all the remained was a wall of thick stone. It would buy them a few more seconds. Anyone pursuing them would have to run to the other side of the ballroom and out a different set of doors.

This time when the prince didn't move, it wasn't because of anything she'd said. It was because of what she'd done.

"You just recoded that?"

"Yeah, so?" Cindira heard the sound of approaching hooves, and turned over her shoulder to see the diminutive human iteration of Laporte sitting in place of a coachman atop the approaching surrey. "I'm a hacker, right? Isn't that what Johanna just told you?"

"Hackers can't rewrite structure on a whim like that."

"I'm a *very good* hacker." She pulled back on his jacket, careful to keep the blade from actually touching his skin. "Move. We don't have much time."

The door of the coach opened the moment Laporte drew the horses to a stop. This time, it was Cindira who was thrown off kilter. Was that an automated process, or had she accomplished the task without even putting the code together this time? She'd have to wonder about that later.

The crowd funneled outside as Cindira lowered the knife, spun the prince, and used the blade to indicate the intended action. To his credit, he didn't seem the slightest bit intimidated. His cool compliance in itself, an act of bravery. Of course, he didn't understand the true threat, so why would he worry? His avatar had been murdered before, and he'd woken up back in his own body in the real.

Just as Cindira got a foothold to step into the coach, Johanna rounded the far corner of the palace, rushing down a cascade of stairs.

"Stop!" she shouted. "You'll never get away with this!"

Cindira pondered the years that passed since her mother's murder, swirled them with the moments since finding her father, and suddenly understood her place in the world.

"It's me who should be saying that to you."

Laporte pulled the reins, and they were off.

THIRTY

FRANCISCO WASN'T SCARED.

He was livid.

And mystified.

And still, livid.

The woman collapsed back against the cushioned bench opposite him like the hard part was over. As the coach fled, she worked the coif over her head with her free hand, letting it fall to the seat beside her, and Francisco got his first unobstructed view of his kidnapper. Her voice had been familiar, but now with her long, black locks framing a face distinguished by high cheekbones, a nose that hooked slightly at the end, and brilliantly sand-hued skin, there could be no doubt.

Two possibilities to explain the impossible: either the woman before him was an impostor, or Omala Grover wasn't dead after all. While that may seem ridiculous, there were stories out there to suggest otherwise. Or maybe even fifteen years later, he still refused to believe a woman of her capabilities could be lost to something as prosaic as a boating mishap. Until he was sure which possibility was true, Francisco had no intention of admitting he recognized the avatar before him. Or at least, its namesake.

She looked him in the eye and guessed immediately at the thoughts running through his mind. "I'm not her."

"Obviously," he said, like it actually was.

"Of course, obviously." A tiny smile tugged at the corner of her lips, like she knew he was putting on a front. "I'm sorry for scaring you."

"I'm not scared."

"Then I'm sorry for pissing you off," she amended. "I did want to talk to you, but that wasn't exactly the way I hoped it'd go down. What I had to say to you, though, I couldn't say in front of Kaylie Fife. The important thing to know is that I have no intention of hurting you."

"Intention only means you haven't conceived of hurting me, not that you've ruled it out completely." Francisco pointed to the knife she held, its handle pressed into her knee, though her grip had eased somewhat. "You might as well stab me and get all the angst out of your system. I'll wake up back in the real where I'll promptly contact Plaxis and have your profile tracked, your jackpod's location revealed, and your ass, arrested."

"I think you'd find that easier said than done." She threw the knife on the seat next to *him*. "Here. If it makes you feel better, you hold it. I only threatened you with it to save you."

He snatched up the weapon while gazing at her with utter incredulity. "In what world do you save someone by putting a knife to their throat?"

"One where the knife is the lesser threat."

Even as the rocking coach sped out of the palace compound, the woman seemed uncertain of how to proceed. She hadn't expected this whole kidnapping thing to work, he theorized, and now that it had, she wasn't sure what to do next. Her chest heaved as she clutched at her hair, and he recognized the mannerisms as ones he himself had displayed whenever stretching his mental capabilities. Finally, she exhaled through pursed lips.

"Okay, so, someone's trying to kill you."

"Besides you?" He feigned shock. "Do tell."

"I don't know much more than that. I don't *know* it at all. But I feel it instinctively, and my instincts are almost never wrong."

Francisco sat back, his eyes focusing on the moonlit scenery whisking by outside. "How easy your life must be with that level of confidence."

"Hardly, people tend to be very disappointing. For once, I'd like to be surprised."

Suddenly, the coach slowed to a stop. Two ticks later, the driver, a diminutive young man looking vaguely Southeast Asian but attired in clothes befitting the Kingdom's baroque European aesthetic, opened the door. He nodded once to Francisco, then turned on the woman across the way.

"Miss, Yuchi went active two minutes ago and is presumably triangulating our position. I have just registered her passing out of the palace zone. I'm scrambling our location as best I can, but you should make haste."

"Already? Damn it, I'm running out of time." She nodded, then turned again on the prince. "Plaxis doesn't have access to the source code. They've been trying for years to get into it, but Omala Grover put up the programming equivalent of a forest of thorns built of Purusha Prime code around it. There's only one living soul who might be able to get through without damaging it, but she must know what your intentions are."

Francisco kept all emotions from his face as he channeled his inner diplomat, even though what he really wanted was to take the knife to *her* throat and get her to talk. "My intentions are classified. But answer me this: why would Plaxis's ability to access the source code be a bad thing?"

"Because then, they'd be unstoppable. This place—" She took on a mocking air. "—this *Kingdom*—is proof they want profit and power over progress. Gaia was supposed to bring the world together. Places like this and the kind of people who patronize it pull it apart. And now that Plaxis has licensed out a derivative of it to so many nations and entities, they're all dependent on it for their welfare. Right now, Plaxis's limitations are all that keep it from being the de factor ruler of the world. If they gain the power of the source code, they could bring every nation of the world to its feet, directly or indirectly."

"Why do you think I'm here? I'm not just a pretty figurehead. I'm the sovereign of the virtual world, and a strong influence on the real one. I'm aware of what the Kingdom really is, and I'm aware of the danger it is even as it makes Gaia possible." He scooted forward on his seat. "Is it you? Are you the one who knows how to get to it?"

"I didn't say anyone *could* get to it. I said someone might be able to, if they truly believed it was necessary."

"And what gives this person the right to have that kind of power?"

She blinked her confusion. "What?"

"You talk about the welfare of humanity and the dangers of totalitarianism, but what could be more typical of a despot than a person who holds the solution to saving Gaia, but refuses to share it because it might also benefit something she detests?"

The woman gazed at him for the longest moment before huffing. "Look, I've said what I came here to say. I have to go. Be on the lookout, your highness. Someone wants you dead. You were a fool to show up here. Don't do it again. I'm not sure if I can get in again to help you, and frankly, I have more important people to save if I can come back."

The mousy man cried out again. "The time, miss."

Not-Omala ignored him. "You have to understand, here isn't like Gaia. You die in the Kingdom, you die in the real." Having dropped that bomb, her message must have been complete. The black-haired woman stood and exited the coach. "I have to go."

"Wait... What?" Francisco hopped out of the coach and gave chase, still clutching the blade she'd surrendered. She was already five feet away, moving as quickly as she could, almost as though she were being hunted. "If that's true, then why give me this—" he held up the knife. "—your only defense? I might have just stuck you with it, thinking all it would do would be to send you out of the program."

She paused and turned back. A smile lifted the corners of her mouth. "Because the kind of man whose instinct it is to save a child from an explosion—even a child he was convinced was an enemy—when he knows neither of them was really in danger, wouldn't stab a defenseless woman, even virtually."

Save a child from an explosion?

"It was you." Francisco's mouth had gone suddenly dry. "Omala? Are you still alive?"

"I've already told you, no."

"But the source code." Who else would possibly know how? "Please, Gaia needs your help. Don't..."

Footfalls rampaged, an angry figure cloaked in black armor and brandishing a sword ran towards them. A samurai? Here? It made no sense. Francisco had no time to dwell on that, however, as the first clang of the bell descended from the clock tower over the palace gates, bringing with it an electrifying chill.

Goooonggg.

Francisco checked the facsimile of his Papa's watch. Midnight.

Not-Omala lashed her head around, her face paling. "What do I do?"

The petite man said, "She'll need to maintain a logistical framework to attack. It will be a disadvantage."

Francisco didn't understand who the samurai was, or why Not-Omala needed to run from her, but he did know the Asian woman across the way had one hell of a sword in her hand, and it made the knife the kidnapper had used look like a spatula. Before he stopped to think otherwise, Francisco threaded his hand through Not-Omala's, and pulled her with all his might. "We have to run!"

Goooonggg.

Their feet pounded, but their pursuer made a mockery of their flight. Lithe steps and swift feet weren't winning; the samurai ate the space between them with each step. It didn't help that whatever shoes Not-Omala had on clanked and clicked with each pump of her legs. All the while, that infernal clock tower rang from afar, reminding them that danger was coming at them from all levels.

Goooonggg.

Not-Omala stopped suddenly, yanking Francisco back and holding out her hand. "Quick, give me the knife!"

Was she crazy? "No, we can make it to the exit!"

She took the blade, despite his protest. "I need to make sure *you're* safe. You're the prince; I'm no one!"

Goooonggg.

"I *need* to get into the source code, before Gaia comes crashing down. If the person you know can help me do that—"

His argument seemed to win her over. Suddenly, her feet began to move.

Goooonggg.

They reached the port. A silver button on the frame of the door pulsed light, one of the few things to behave in a non-era conforming way in the platform. Francisco's hand smashed down, and inside his head, an internal countdown clock began to tick off the five-second delay required before jumping.

Five... Four....

Three... Two...

"No!"

Just as his foot fell forward, her hand left his.

Francisco spun and found disaster: the samurai, her left arm braced around not-Omala's neck, with the sword pushed against the base of his kidnapper's throat. A drop of blood trickled down from where the blade nicked her.

The samurai's speech held no accent. "Back away from the gate, Your Majesty."

Goooonggg.

Not-Omala's hands clutched around her captor's arm, but proved powerless to free herself, Not-Omala's lip quivered. "Don't listen to her. Go!"

His head swiveled between the situation before him and the exit behind him. "But she'll kill you."

"Think! I'm out at midnight, but why would she want you to stay?"

Goooonggg.

He'd been so wrapped up in the danger before him, he'd failed to anticipate that to come. Not-Omala made a good point: He was not only a free citizen, but the Prince of Gaia. What reason would this – she must be a security bot of some kind?– have for forcing his presence at such dire stakes if not for an ulterior motive?

And who was the woman held captive, that the samurai didn't just slay her on sight?

Someone who was of value to his enemies as well.

Someone... who knew how to access the source code.

Goooonggg.

Francisco looked upon the woman with newfound reverence. "It *is* you."

"Your Majesty—" The samurai's blade bit deeper, bringing a trickle chasing the path of the previous single drop. It must have hurt, but Not-Omala did nothing more than suck in a breath. "I must insist."

What could he do? *What could he do?* He couldn't let this woman die, and he couldn't succumb to threats.

But before he could act on his own, before he could even decide what to do, his options were taken away from him.

Not-Omala groaned, throwing all her weight back. The heel of her translucent shoe sped his direction. Instinct drove Francisco. Sensing an attack, he tried to catch her blow before it connected. All he managed was to get a hold of one of her curious slippers, which came off in his hands as the force of the maneuver threw him off balance and falling backward.

A moment was all it took for the samurai's sword to fall between them, slicing into Francisco's wrist just as his body passed through the portal.

Red everywhere.

Blood in his eyes.

Dead eyes staring into his soul.

"BREATHE, YOUR MAJESTY! Breathe!"

His eyelids shot up, but the sight didn't bring clarity. All around him, Gaia security forces swarmed. He was still in his jackpod, but the lid had been lifted away. A pressure on his wrist forced him to pull his arm up to examine it, out of a physician's hands.

"Your Majesty! Wait." The woman yanked his arm back under her control. "Let me clean it. We'll get you to a medical suite as soon as we staunch the bleeding. Try to stay calm."

"Bleeding? I—"

His words tapered off where his confusion took over.

The physician looked up just long enough to grimace. "You just reached down and scratched your own arm to hell. You're going to need sutures."

"How? I was jacked in. How did I get injured while I was—"

But then it all came rushing back to him: the ball, the confrontation with Hugo, the kidnapping, the samurai.

The woman.

Francisco's head lashed to the side, finding two members of his tech team hovering on the periphery of the bubble about him. "The woman who abducted me. Who was she?"

They looked at each other in confusion. "Abduction?"

Of course, they wouldn't know. Anyone else at the ball would have had to leave the palace to exit as well. No chance Carlos had yet gotten back to reveal the emergency within, and his security officers only had tangential access to the Kingdom's monitoring system to observe.

No matter. Soon enough, the whole world would know.

Francisco yanked back his hand, pulling the damaged arm into his chest, and sat up, despite his physician's protestations.

"Find her!" He shouted. "I don't care what it takes, just find her!"

THIRTY-ONE

Any relief Cindira felt at seeing Francisco's form fall into a darkened doorway and, presumably, out of the platform evaporated when the tip of Yuchi's sword pierced her skin.

"Laporte?" Cindira's eyes moved in the direction of the fidgeting figure to the right. "What do I do?"

"I've determined the best option is to fight your way out."

The involuntary guffaw that erupted from her chest would have been funny any other time. "Seriously? Why can't you just do whatever you did back in the castle and force her to restart?"

Goooonggg.

"Because she's adapted to my attack; it wouldn't work a second time." Laporte came to her aid, pulling Cindira to her feet.

"Enough of your chattering!" Yuchi's hand flew out. If the dagger had been on her person somewhere, or if she'd conjured it out of air on a whim, Cindira couldn't say. Her aim, however, was true.

"Laporte!"

Just as he'd done in the palace, the botic disappeared. This time, however, not into thin air. He let out one very terrified shriek as he dissolved into a mouse and scurried away to safety underneath a nearby water trough. The knife hit a rock and tumbled to the ground near Cindira's feet.

Goooonggg.

Her shouting achieved nothing. It was too late.

As the resonance of the last bell dissipated, Cindira closed her eyes and accepted the inevitable. She would be booted out of the Kingdom. Would it kill her? Would it hurt? Would it somehow reveal her true identity? All these answers lay on the other side of midnight.

Only, nothing happened. She was still jacked in. She cracked open her eyes and looked down at her legs pressed into the ground before her. She no longer wore the servant attire. Her hands pressed to her face, recognizing not her mother, but her own.

With no one else to ask, Cindira took her question to the security bot at the other end of the sword aimed for her chest. "Why are you stopping?"

Yuchi still held out her sword. "You are to wait here; I am to wait with you."

"Wait?" Cindira scooted back, only for Yuchi to advance in her retreat. "For what?"

"An override to your rejection was ordered by the Queen. You will be detained until she arrives." Her weapon remained fixed. "You will not be harmed as long as you are compliant."

The scenario played out in Cindira's mind in the snap of a second: Johanna's arrival, being discovered for who she really was, her stepmother's realization that she had confessed to Omala's own daughter the murder she'd committed. The possibility that a magic-wielding, world-controlling Johanna may decide it would be easier to kill Cindira here and cover up yet another death.

No, she couldn't let that happen. She must live. She must avenge her mother. She must save her father. She must protect Gaia.

"That's where you're wrong." Cindira kneeled down, feeling the stem of the knife press into her hand. "I've been compliant all my life, and the *only* thing it's done is bring me harm."

Eyes shifting, grin lifting, the bot followed Cindira's movement like a cat sizing its prey. "You don't really think you can take me, can you?"

"I can't defeat you, but I don't need to. The only thing I *need* to do is get through that portal."

She's doing here what I do in the Stadium, Cindira thought. *And if she can do that without knowing what I know, what couldn't I do if I tried?* The Kingdom wasn't reality. The vreal was a creation of a genius but human mind, and AI or no, a human mind could rule it, change it, command it. Hadn't she already done it once tonight? Changing a door to a wall was a simple swapping of attributes. That's all everything was here: a pasting together of attributes and code commands and intention.

Her right arm lashed out, while her mind strung together the code to render what she'd imagined. Yuchi took a step back when the dagger disappeared, and a rapier replaced it.

"You... You recoded it. While inside the platform! Impossible!"

Cindira kept her focus, lifting the sword back, to the right, to the ready. "We don't have to do this. Just let me leave."

The samurai mirrored the pose. "I cannot permit it."

Confusion. Noise. Strength. Fear. The swing of the katana brought them all in Cindira's direction.

She leapt back. Once. Twice. Volley. Block. Thrust.

Cindira fought with the might of the woman she was, and the child she'd been. Every strike, blocked. Every parry, met with equal rebuttal. Being able to conjure a sword out of nothing *was* impressive, but it was not indominable. Yuchi settled both her hands on her sword, rounding with a barbarous yelp in a spinning blow.

"Stand down!" Yuchi bellowed. "I will not harm you unless driven to do so."

Unless driven to do so...

Laporte's words echoed in her mind. *"She'll need to maintain a logistical framework to attack. It will be a disadvantage."*

If that was true, that meant Yuchi was subject to the same rules Cindira was. But whereas Yuchi was a creature born of code, who could only carry out programming and act on protocol, Cindira was not.

The katana fell away as the earth below the samurai's feet bubbled and stewed. A few lines of the program altered, inserted by Cindira's thoughts into the Kingdom's programming as a limited application. She'd made a sandbox of the place where Yuchi stood, and filled it with quicksand.

Cindira wasted no time. Jumping to her feet, she realized suddenly why her balance felt so uneven. One of her shoes was missing. Only, where was it?

The clop-clop of horse hooves filtered through the air, and she knew she'd have to leave it behind. It was only a vreal manifestation of the glass slipper, after all. Surely its absence didn't imply anything more.

Eyes on the gate, Cindira dropped the sword in her hand, and threw herself forward, into to the exit portal.

THIRTY-TWO

JOHANNA STEWED. FROM her office high above the city, her eyes catalogued the skyline that stretched from Twin Peaks, down to where parts of the old city had been reclaimed by the tides. Across the Bay, Oakland and Berkeley twinkled, almost as if Omala, rotting in her grave, managed to laugh at her.

A knock on her door broke her reverie.

"Yes?"

Her assistant peeked around the corner. "Your daughter is here to see you, Ms. Tieg."

Her eyes closed, both against the view, and against the annoyance of her insipid child's whining about being upstaged by a hacker. "Tell Kaylie I'll come by her office in a little while."

Willa took two steps into the office. "Not *that* daughter."

"I only have one—"

Johanna cut herself off the moment she realized what the assistant meant. She sent the comque moments before, a request to Cindira to meet and discuss heightened security protocols. Covering up what had happened two nights ago in the Kingdom proved impossible; there were far too many witnesses. Damage control meant that Johanna had to spend every moment since conferencing with VIP clients, convincing them not to cancel their memberships, that no harm would come to them. Hackers had only gotten inside the platform three times in its history. Each breach was an opportunity for improvement. Now, the platform was even more secure than it had been before, she told them.

Most of them fell for her excuses.

Some did not.

She needed to make sure that she wasn't just blowing smoke up the asses of those who'd agreed to stay members. Cindira was the best coder Plaxis had. The best coder anywhere, perhaps. For the company to survive this, Omala Grover's meek little daughter had a lot of work before her.

"Cindira? Already?"

The assistant confirmed it with a nod. "Did you want me to tell her to come back in a little while?"

"No, I—" Johanna smoothed out her jacket and cleared her throat. "Show her in."

Johanna couldn't remember when she'd started hating her step-daughter. No matter what anyone claimed, it had not been since their first meeting. In fact, Johanna had been rather taken by the beautiful, precocious, and vastly intelligent eight-year-old child. So much so, that she envied Omala for her fortune.

But no matter how hard Johanna tried to win Cindira's heart, it was not to be done. Oh, the girl had never been disrespectful. On the contrary, Rex's child from his first marriage was gracious to a fault. After a while, that wore on Johanna. And, oh, how Rex doted on her. Who was this child to treat her cordially and distantly at the same time?

No, hate had not come first. First it was confusion, then bitterness. And then, jealousy. Jealousy when Johanna understood that Rex would always love his daughter so much more than he loved her, and that this daughter was so much like her mother that...

Well, when put that way, it seemed silly, but such was the human heart. Omala's death had been the perfect opportunity, it turned out, to exorcise Cindira from their lives. "Everything here will remind her of her mother," she'd told Rex. "She'll constantly be brought down by reminders at every turn. And she's so intelligent. Kaylie and Cade? They tease and taunt, and she doesn't deserve that. Boarding school is really the best thing for her now."'

Rex bought into the "mother's insight" line. *Such a fool.*

A fool she hadn't planned on loving but managed it anyhow. And now, she might lose him too.

"Surely you've heard about what happened." Plaxis's commander kept her eyes turned to the city outside the windows as her step-daughter crossed the distance between the door and the chair in front of the desk with tentative, measured steps.

Cindira's tiny, unsure voice answered, "The prince, kidnapped.

They say he's okay though. I read that some mysterious woman managed to hack her way into the program."

Johanna turned her glare up to eleven. "We don't know if it was a woman." Johanna had suspicions, but none she planned to share in current company. "The avatar used belonged to a woman, but it, too, was hijacked. We should assume nothing about the hacker unless we have firm proof of his or her attributes."

The girl's eyes raced to the floor. "Of course." Then, barely looking up, she added. "How do you know the avatar was hijacked?"

"Because who it belonged to...there's no way that person could really be there. It's impossible."

Luckily, Cindira pressed no further, only nodding and looking back to her feet.

Johanna turned her attention back to the matter at hand. "So far, most of the press has accepted my explanation: the whole thing was a test to see if our security measures were as effective as we claimed them to be. They failed, and one rogue hacker was able to take advantage of the situation." Johanna leaned forward, her voice lowering. "But you and I know that's not what really happened, don't we?"

The young thing flushed. She never could take an authoritative tone well. "We do?"

"Yes, we do. Your mother was a genius. What, does it surprise you to hear me say that? You think I didn't respect her talents? She was a luminary, and you were her little doppelganger from the very first time I met you."

Cindira stayed maddeningly quiet.

Johanna smashed her palm against the desk. "Enough is enough, already. Admit you know how to access the source code, and then *do it*. Genius or no, we need to tap into the root directories and fortify the Kingdom, or it's all going to fall apart."

"But I keep telling you, I don't know how to get *into* the source code."

"Find a way. Clean up this mess! If you don't—"

It would sound like a threat, and for once, Johanna didn't want that. But what else could she say? It was the truth.

"If you don't," the blonde's chest fell as she exhaled, "then you're probably going to be an orphan very soon."

Cindira looked like a caught fish trying to understand how she'd ended up on land. "I'm sorry?"

Now that the can of worms was open, nothing remained but to bait the hook. "Your father isn't traveling. He's been kidnapped. Kidnapped, sound familiar? The same tactic used by the hacker who broke into the Kingdom. I don't doubt they are one in the same."

For a girl who harped on about the inability to reach her father for months, Cindira took the news with amazing poise. "Is that so?"

Perhaps the estrangement between daughter and father she'd long sought had come to pass unnoticed.

"It is," Johanna continued. "His avatar is laying in stasis in the Kingdom, under my care. I can't track the connection, can't break him free. For two months now, Cindira. Even in the best of circumstances, how much longer can I expect his real-world body to endure?"

"But why would someone kidnap my father? For money?"

"If they wanted money, they would have made demands by now. What they want is power. What they want...is the source code."

There was the reaction she'd been looking for: shock, confusion, disappointment, fear.

Especially fear.

"But anyone who has the source code for the Kingdom has the source code for Gaia. They could destroy everything my mother built, and in the process, release war back into the real."

"If we want to save your father, what choice do we have?"

"It's not a choice," Cindira argued. "They want something we can't give them."

"They want something we can't give them *yet*." Johanna settled into her seat, and into her decision to press forward. "You are the single most talented code writer of your generation, and your skills don't stop there. Rumor has it that you show up in the hackdomes, and that you are undefeated."

The girl's eyes went to the floor as she shook her head. "I'm not sure I know what you mean."

"Like hell you don't. Cade saw you there a few weeks ago. For that offense alone, I could fire you, but I also know you're the best hope we have to save your father. You don't care about me, and we both know how I feel about you, but what about him? Won't you finally admit you know the code for *him*?"

Cindira kept her silence, but the guilt weighing down her features only emboldened Johanna.

"You have the skills. Use them!" she drove on. "Break into the source code. We can clean up the damage once he's safe."

"But what you're asking me to do is basically dismantle my mother's legacy."

"To save the life of the man we both love!" Johanna labored to tone down her rising voice. "You do love your father, don't you? You even changed your name after your mother died to honor him."

Now she flashed red. "Of course, I love my father." And behind her eyes, Johanna read the unspoken allegation, *far more than you do*.

"Then help me. Draw out the people who've done this, and once they've crawled out of the shadows, we'll cut them down, once and for all."

THIRTY-THREE

LAPORTE WISHED HE HAD the ability to listen in to the real the way he could the vreal. He could tunnel through tech, become a bug that wormed its way right into any other system around, but analysis suggested detection too likely. The events of two nights before had forced every security specialist Plaxis had to report for duty. There were so many new tripwires being laid down in the code, even a mouse would have trouble not stumbling over them.

The door flew open, followed by a blur of blue cotton and black hair. Cindira didn't stop to speak. She went straight to the bathroom of the small pool house she and Asla shared and slammed the door behind her. A moment later came the sounds of retching.

Laporte's patience could rival a mountain's most days, but he found himself...curious. He tried to tell himself it was a result of programming, that it was merely the intersection of new knowledge and his lack of it. But there was something more there. Concern? That was a human emotion. Machines were meant to be impartial. His programming gave him a mission, not the other way around.

Finally, after several minutes, his master reemerged, pale as a sheet and with strands of hair stuck to her face.

"Miss?"

She held up a hand as she struggled to the couch, collapsing the moment she arrived. "I'm stronger now. I'm not afraid of her. I shouldn't have..." But she cut herself off.

"You shouldn't have listened to me." He'd finally spent enough time with Cindira to train his predictive speech pattern algorithms. "I know it could not have been easy, facing the woman who admitted to murdering your mother without tipping your hand, but it was necessary. If you make yourself an enemy of Johanna Tieg right now, you'll draw away from her ability to protect your father. In weakening her, you'd only strengthen whomever is keeping Rex a prisoner. You must continue your charade and work with Plaxis until they're brought down. And you must protect Gaia."

"Protect Gaia!" Cindira laughed as she slicked her hair off her forehead. "How can *I* protect Gaia?"

"Don't you want to?"

Her mouth gaped. "Of course, I do, but how? Even if I make myself a new avatar and hack in—or somehow trace the one that appeared as if by magic in the Kingdom — what can I really do there?"

"You can listen." The mouse jumped up onto the coffee table to be eye-to-eye with her. "Miss, since your mother died, you've been made to feel invisible. You've been a footnote in the ledger of your own family. Sent to boarding school, while your stepsiblings were being loved in a house with your father. Forced to work under Kaylie's direction at Plaxis all while she took credit for your work and abused your talents for her own gain. You've experienced nothing but the disadvantages of not being seen."

Laporte pulled himself up to as much height as his tiny body would offer. "But now it's time to realize, if they never look your way, they never see you coming."

She wiped away the tears from her cheeks and nodded. "You're saying, keep the status quo."

"As far as they know it, yes" Laporte clarified. "Cast out your roots under the ground, so when you break the soil, you're in too deep to be swept away."

"You know, for a programmed entity, you have a great grasp on metaphor." She sat up. "You're right, but I'm just one person versus the whole system. I'm really good at what I do, but how can that ever be enough?"

It was time. "You're not alone, miss. There are others inside the Plaxis systems who are ready to help you. One saved you in the arena, and again at the ball, shielding you from sight until you no longer needed it."

"I wondered how that happened." Cindira shifted in place. "Who is this person who helped me?"

A mouse couldn't smile, but Laporte wasn't just any mouse. "Let's just call her your fairy godmother."

A MESSAGE FROM KENDRAI

I really, really hope you enjoyed *Mistress of Cinders*. It is so different from anything I've written before (not a single kiss in the book AT ALL! Don't worry if that's what you're looking for. Book two will have kissing.) As an indie author without the backing of a large publisher or huge marketing budget, my biggest career challenge is gaining visibility in this booming industry. As a reader, I hope the entertainment you got from reading the book encourages you to be part of Team Meeks, so that I can continue to bring future fairytale-inspired urban fantasy and science fiction books to your bookshelves. Readers often ask me in what way they can help, and here are a few quick, easy things that, while small, are powerful:

- Leave a review. Whether that's on the venue where you purchased this book, on a community reader site like Reddit or Goodreads, or on a blog, every bit is appreciated.

- Tell a book friend. Recs are one of the main ways I discover new books, and hope you do too.

- Visit my website to join the reader newsletter. It will help you stay aware of new releases, events I'll be appearing at, and other news. Also, I tend to do a lot of giveaways. (You get your first such giveaway right after joining the list.)

- Join my reader group on Facebook.

- For advanced practitioners: offer a goat sacrifice to a pagan spirit. Note: I can't condone *actual* goat sacrifice, so in lieu of that, I'd advise Haagan-Dazs or Ben & Jerry's ice cream eaten to bring glory to the 1980s rock idol of your choice. (If you *do* do this, I need pictures people. PICTURES.)

ACKNOWLEDGMENTS

To my author buds who listen to me complain and keep me accountable to my own goals: the Merry Martones and Elizabeth Hunter.

To my editor, Rebecca, who modeled this block of misshaped clay into something that would not only hold water, but a variety of other liquids.

To my ARC team, who provided me feedback and support.

To my kids who continue to be understanding on the nights when we have to eat pizza. Yes, again.

To my (ex) bosses, who, after twenty years of employment, told me to go be a writer already, with their blessings.

To all my parents, biological and spiritual, who continue to support all that I do, by choice or by necessity.

MEEKSOLOGY

RED CHRONICLES
Requited
Reluctant
Relinquished
Ravening
Rebellious
Righteous

RED ORIGINS
Beauty & the Betrayer
The Wolf & the Watcher
Red & the Restorer

ENTER THE KINGDOM
Court of Discontent
Freebird: An Enter the Kingdom side story novella
Mistress of Cinders
Isle of After

VAMPIRE SOVEREIGNS
Venice Dusk